AWAKENED

THE ORACLE CHRONICLES
BOOK I

BY

MONI BOYCE

LOVE
SNACKS
PUBLISHING

Love Snacks Publishing, LLC

Awakened: The Oracle Chronicles © 2019 Shaquana M. Boyce

www.lovesnackspublishing.com

First Edition
ISBN: 978-0-9980436-7-8

Book cover design by: Mallory Rock of Rock Solid Book Design

AWAKENED

CHAPTER 1

Willow

IN THE SEVENTEEN years he'd haunted her dreams, she never knew his name. The flattering, tailor-made, charcoal gray suit he wore accentuated his well-defined body. His dark hair brushed the top of his collar. He had a commanding presence and a regal bearing which seemed fitting since he sat atop a lavish, golden throne. The only thing missing was a crown.

Upon first glimpse, the smile and the outward man might have fooled many, but her subconscious knew underneath that lurked an abominable darkness that longed to capture her. His intense, cold eyes smiled at her. The green depths held a ferociousness that frightened her. His look was what she envisioned Ted Bundy's expression must have looked like to his victims right before he changed from a handsome stranger to a murderous butcher. His predatory gaze never left her face.

Even though he spoke no words, there was something in his face that beckoned her closer. Her brain told her to flee, but her limbs moved like someone else had command of her body. A silent scream raged in her head. She needed to get as far away from this monster as possible.

Instead, she proceeded as if in a trance. While her stiff legs carried her nearer, she couldn't fight the intimidation and thrill his mere presence evoked. Just before she was in touching distance, he stood and spoke. The sound of his voice, both enticed and frightened her.

"Willow."

She awoke, floundering, her sweaty limbs tangled in the sheets, afraid the man had ensnared her. Kicking against the constraints, she vowed he wouldn't take her without a fight. A feral scream erupted from her throat and she continued to struggle. Minutes later, her eyes blinked open. When she realized she was staring up at her bedroom ceiling, she sat up, clutching the sheet to her chest. The hot, damp sheets clung to her fevered skin. Willow's lungs tried to suck in oxygen. Her heart beat a rapid tattoo against her ribcage.

After a moment, her breathing under control, she pushed her damp, coily curls back from her face and looked around the room. She half-expected to find the sinister man from her dreams lurking in the shadows or corners waiting to finish the possession he had begun in her dream.

These nightmares left her feeling like a wrung out dishrag; frayed nerves and unable to return to sleep.

She exhaled a slow, unsteady breath. Her body still trembled. The dreams had plagued her since she was a child. In all those years, he never aged. He'd also never spoken her name. She'd assumed he didn't know it, which comforted her. It always seemed like he was trying to possess her body. But now he knew her name, and it felt like he came closer to possessing her soul. The evil gleam in his eyes when he'd whispered her name had her on edge.

"It's just a dream. It's just a dream." She said, chanting the mantra that usually soothed her. But not this time. Something about it was so real. She looked over at her digital, alarm clock and the glowing numbers showed it was after five in the morning.

A dull ache began in the back of her head. It could become a full-blown migraine or stay a tolerable headache. She could manage the latter, but the agonizing migraines she often suffered left her debilitated, sometimes for days.

After a few more reassuring looks around the room, her heart rate returned to normal. Her shaking ceased once her eyes landed on Max, her faithful companion. The Northern Inuit dog had been with her for several years, ever since he'd wandered over to her in the park and claimed her as his own. A fleeting temptation to take him to a shelter passed once she looked into his eyes. She was thankful she'd kept him. Wherever he was she felt safe.

She leaned across the bed and ran her hand over his soft, black fur. His ears went up in alert at her touch and for the first time since she woke up, she smiled. Max's right ear, covered in white fur, was the only part of his coat that wasn't shiny black and she found it adorable.

He lifted his head and peered at her. Sometimes she was sure he understood her or sensed her moods, but that was more than likely just a fanciful thought.

"It's okay boy. Go back to sleep. No sense in both of us getting up at this ungodly hour." She rubbed his ears and then got out of bed.

When she entered the bathroom, she turned on the light. In response, a stabbing pain pierced her eyes and temples.

Bad idea.

She flipped the light off again. The moonlight streaming through the window had to be enough. Spots now danced behind her eyelids and caused the throbbing in her head to increase. She looked down at her arm and saw it riddled with goosebumps and covered in sweat that glistened against her sepia brown skin. She turned on the faucet and cupped her hands beneath the cool, running water and drank, taking no heed of the overflow that soaked her t-shirt.

It was three hours before she needed to be ready for work, but sleep was no longer an option. Besides, the thought of another bad dream made her uneasy.

After a long shower meant to soothe her throbbing head, she headed to her favorite coffee shop. Matty, the owner's teenage daughter greeted her.

"Hey Willow! You're here early." Without asking what she wanted, the girl turned to make the usual, a caramel macchiato.

"I could say the same for you. Don't you have school?" She leaned on the counter.

"It's a teacher workday today, so no school. I came in to help Mom." She finished making the sweet coffee drink and passed the cup to Willow.

"Good morning!"

Willow looked up and smiled at the beautiful Hispanic woman that entered from the kitchen.

"Morning Zora!"

It was clear Matty inherited her mother's height and natural beauty. However, Matty's skin was fairer with pink undertones, Zoriana's was a tawny beige. Matty had lush, dark brown wavy curls that fell to the middle of her back. Zoriana's hair was straight and as black as onyx. She often wore it in a long braid. Besides their stature, the other thing that linked the two women was their identical facial features. The pert noses, the arch of their brows and the bow-shaped lips were the same on each woman.

"You're early this morning." Zora watched her with concern.

"It's nothing." Willow looked away and sipped her macchiato. She checked her watch, knowing she had plenty of time before she had to be at work. "I should get going." There was no rush, but the dream had made her antsy... eager to move on, as if loitering too long would invite the sleep-invading man to breach her waking hours.

Zora nodded, but the concern never left.

"See ya later." Matty waved to her and turned to help another customer.

Willow felt crappy for lying and blowing off Zora, who'd been nothing but nice to her. If she was honest, she was always uncomfortable when Zora's probing eyes sought to discern what was wrong. Months ago, she wanted to confide in her. When she tried to tell her about the dreams her pulse raced and her tongue stuck to the roof of her mouth. She'd been afraid Zora would think she was crazy or a head case, if she told her there was a man in her dreams that seemed real. Instead, she remained silent about the boogeyman that haunted her in her nightmares.

Rather than walk into her dead-end job at the collection call center thirty minutes early, she headed to a nearby park where she drank her coffee. From a bench, she watched joggers, moms pushing baby strollers and other pedestrians headed to offices or off to wherever their day was taking them. People watching reminded her of her mother. When she was a child, they would sit in the park and her mom would make up silly stories about the men and women who passed them. The memory elicited a wistful smile. She finished her coffee and tossed the cup before heading to work.

The job sucked, but it paid decent money and gave her the nights and weekends to pursue a career as a singer. Five years, she'd been in Nashville pursuing her passion for music and many told her that her voice was a nice mixture of country and blues. She was fortunate to play frequent open mic nights, at The Bluebird and Douglas Corner Cafe. But, despite the praise of her sultry rasp, no record producers had come calling yet. Or even responded to the audition tapes she had rained on their offices. Maybe it was time to call it quits and admit a music career wasn't in the cards for her. Then again, quitters never succeed. She had a gig in a few days. Anything could happen.

Inside the large room that took up the whole fifth floor, the flickering fluorescent bulbs pounded at her eyeballs. As always, the atmosphere made her feel like it was sucking the life out of her body. She sat and rubbed her throbbing eyes.

After she put on her headset, and placed her first call, the day dragged on.

"Hi, I'm calling from Paradigm Financial Solutions for Frank Wilson."

The words chipped away another piece of her soul. Most people either didn't bother to answer, or they just hung up on you. Every now and then, she got a gem who bitched at her because somehow it was her fault they were delinquent on their bill. She sighed and waited to see which delight this customer would be.

A few hours later, she took a break to stretch and found her gorgeous, but snobby co-worker, Eli Walker, staring. This wasn't the first time she'd caught him.

His blue eyes burned into her and he refused to look away. He never spoke to her and didn't even seem to like her.

Why is he always watching me with his judgy eyes?

A year ago, she had approached him in the break room. A simple hello and an attempt to be friendly, met with his fixed attention on his coffee, followed by a stare similar to the one he was giving her now. Without a word, he'd walked off and left her standing by the vending machine like a dorky schoolgirl who had unsuccessfully tried to gain the attention of the coolest guy in class. Her co-worker always seemed to give her a look that said she wasn't good enough. For what, she didn't know. Maybe it was just in her head. Ever since his lack of a response that day, she felt animosity towards him because she had liked him and he rejected her.

She wished again that management had set up cubicle walls that allowed for privacy, but the company was too cheap to do that. Now, was the perfect time for a bathroom break.

In the last few minutes, her headache had morphed to a full migraine. She stood and stumbled. Her eyes watered and the pain and pressure banged a discordant beat against the inside of her skull. She walked to the restroom without drawing attention to herself and braced herself against the wall. Her vision blurred when she tried to glance around. Even though she was having trouble seeing, she sensed she was the only one in the hallway. She opened her mouth to call for help when a sunburst of pain exploded behind her eyes.

CHAPTER 2

Eli

THE OTHERS ASSIGNED to watch Willow Stevens told Eli she referred to him as The Snob. It was the reason; he tried to keep his distance and avoid looking at her. Sometimes she caught him; like this morning.

He wouldn't have acknowledged her leaving for the bathroom, but the text he received from one of the others put him on alert. When he looked at her a few minutes ago, she seemed troubled.

Was it a migraine?

She got those often. He could count the days last month that she missed work because of them.

Previously, he'd simply just watched and followed her around, staying in the shadows. He'd been okay when they told him to keep his distance, only observe and protect, no communication. Over a year ago, his assignment on the mission changed to co-worker. Even though he led the team, it was the Council that made the decision on their roles during the mission. They changed his role, but the no communication rule was still firm. Other members of the team got to interact with her. Not him.

He didn't fully understand, he'd sworn the oath the same as the others. Was the Council afraid he wouldn't honor the commandment? He shoved away the voice that told him they should be worried. There were times he found himself concerned over his growing feelings for her, but then he reminded himself of his duty. He always got back on track.

Pushing the troubling thought away, he placed his headset on the desk and stepped into the hallway expecting to find it empty. Instead, he found Willow unconscious on the ground. He rushed to her body and felt for a pulse. His touch didn't rouse her. Her flawless brown skin that was usually vibrant was now ashen. It alarmed him.

It was against protocol, but he needed to get her to a safe place. Something besides the migraine had caused the blackout. He wasn't certain, but he had a hunch. He picked her up in his arms and looked at her face once more before they both vanished.

***

Eli's apartment was a converted loft that used to be an old industrial space. The interior boasted exposed brick walls, pipes that ran along the ceiling and cement floors. His furnishings and decor were sparse. The minute they appeared in his living room, he took her to his bedroom and laid her on the bed.

Over the last few years, he watched over her and learned more about her. Despite his attempts not to, he'd fallen...

Don't say the word.

He couldn't. It was forbidden. Even though that was the case, his eyes never left her. Her natural curls lay across the pillow in a myriad of directions. Her full, plump lips looked like they were aching to be kissed. Color was returning to her high cheekbones.

He sat on the edge of the bed and caressed her cheek. The pulse beat in her slender neck. His fingers traced over the necklace she always wore. It held a silver pendant of a dangling, slithering Python. On further inspection, the intricate detail of the jewelry showed it may have been an antique. A small whimper escaped her lips, and he jerked his hand away, afraid of being caught. After giving her one last look, he left the bedroom.

In the living room, he paced the floor. He'd broken the rules by bringing her here. The Council had forbidden him to have contact with her unless they gave consent. Every minute, he turned his head toward his bedroom where she rested. There was no way he could keep what he did from the others. They had a right to know. He pulled out his phone and sent a group text.

Within seconds, a tall dark-skinned black woman with long dreadlocks and a tattoo sleeve up her left arm appeared in his kitchen.

"Is this true?" She hissed. "She's here?" Her dreadlocks whipped back and forth while her eyes darted around the loft looking for Willow. "Elias, what are you going to tell her when she wakes up in your apartment? Better yet, what are you going to tell the Council when they ask why you broke the rules?"

Eli defended himself against Phaedra's verbal attack. "I didn't have a choice."

Before he had time to elaborate, Zora and Matty appeared in the living room. Both wore concerned expressions. They were about to question him.

He held up his hand to stop them. "Zoriana, Mathilda, let everyone arrive and then I will explain."

Both women shut their mouths and sat on the couch. Phaedra prowled the room in anger.

A minute later, a petite blonde with a pixie cut appeared in the living room. "There better be a good explanation why Willow is in your apartment. What were you thinking bringing her here?" She folded her arms across her chest.

"Eli said he would explain when everyone was here. We were waiting for you, Morgana." Zora spoke to the woman, but her eyes never left Eli.

He ignored the hostile looks he was receiving, while he awaited another member of the team. "Just give me a few more minutes. We're expecting one more."

"Who?" Morgan looked at Zora and Matty confused. They returned her expression with an equally perplexed one.

"Max." Eli and Phaedra said in unison. Both glanced at each other. Zora, Matty and Morgan shared a look.

"Who is he?"

"Why is he a part of this?"

"Nobody told us."

The questions flew at them. Phaedra looked to Eli to offer the group answers.

"It wasn't my decision not to tell you. Take it up with the Council." The doorbell rang, saving him from a further interrogation. When he answered the door, a tall Asian man with longish black hair that had a shock of white running through it stepped inside the room. Despite being clothed, it was obvious he was in great physical shape, since his body was a dead ringer for Brad Pitt's body in *Fight Club*. His clothing looked like he'd gotten dressed in the dark.

Matty eyed him from head to toe.

"I was in a rush." He shrugged and moved further into

the room, where he came to stand next to Phaedra.

"Okay, now that everyone is here..."

"Wait. Are you going to tell us why he's here?" Morgan turned accusing eyes on Max.

Eli looked at Phaedra and she nodded her head. "Max is a werewolf."

The collective gasp from the other women, made Eli rub the back of his neck in frustration and sigh. "This isn't the first time we've worked with other supernaturals."

"It's just that the Protectors never included anyone, but witches." Zora glared at Max with hostile curiosity. "How do we know we can trust him?"

"We can trust him." Phaedra slipped her hand into Max's.

He smiled at her. His fingers squeezed hers in return.

"Once upon a time you found love outside our community." Phaedra stared Zora in the eyes, causing her to wipe the disapproval from her face.

Matty cast her eye at her mother looking for answers. Zora looked away and bristled at Phaedra's comments.

"Enough. We don't have time for bickering." Eli stuffed his hands deep into his pockets and stopped pacing to stare at everyone. "I had to bring Willow here. She passed out at work. I think something caused the migraine..." He paused while the group took in the information. "I believe Killian is behind it." When everyone spoke at once, he raised his hands in a gesture for silence. "We have to tell her."

"Are you crazy?" Morgan looked around for someone to agree with her.

"Eli, it's against the Protector Commandment to reveal to her who she is." Zora tried to be the voice of reason.

There was no other way if Willow was in danger. "You know what Killian is capable of. What if her migraines are getting worse because he's trying harder to find her?" As everyone considered what he said, he pushed on with his plan. "I think we have to tell her who she is and prepare her."

"Prepare her how? What do you mean?" Phaedra asked, but he could see in her eyes she knew what he meant.

"We have to train her. Get her ready, because he's coming for her and she needs to be able to defend herself."

Everyone talked over each other. Eli tried to get one last thing in before everything descended into chaos. "If we train her and teach her she might defeat him."

It was too late. His words fell on deaf ears. They yelled over each other, trying to be heard.

"What is going on?" Willow's voice rose above the den of shouting voices.

Startled, after hearing her, they turned to gape at her. Willow's bewildered gaze swept the room. Eli chastised himself for not keeping them quiet. He hadn't intended for her to wake up and find everyone here.

CHAPTER 3

Willow

"YOU'RE AN ORACLE."

What does he mean?

Her brain was still trying to wrap itself around waking up in an apartment that wasn't hers, among a mixture of people in her life she hadn't been aware even knew each other. When she walked into the living room and found Zora and Matty that owned the coffee shop; Morgan, her neighbor she hung out with occasionally; Phaedra, a bartender that worked a bar where she performed; Eli, her snobby, gorgeous co-worker and a random guy who seemed familiar arguing, it baffled her. What were they all doing there? What was she doing here?

Despite the tension and obvious disapproval from the rest of the group, Eli had spent the last twenty minutes telling her about some superhuman skill she had and that a vampire was after her.

"So let me get this straight..." She took a deep breath. "The women in my family can see the future. We're the only ones in the world with this power... You guys are part of a group called the Protectors..." She looked around the room at each of them. A few of them nodded to confirm her statement. "Your mission has always been to protect the 'Oracle.'" She used air quotes when she said the word, Oracle. "That something or someone you've been protecting me from is the King of the Vampires... the man named Killian." She gulped and her eyes landed back on Eli. "And you're witches." She swallowed once more while she tried to digest everything.

"Well, everyone, but me. I'm a werewolf." Max beamed when he shared the news like that made any of this sound less strange.

She nodded, but then something clicked in her brain.

"Max?" She looked at him with new clarity and her mouth fell open. He said he was a werewolf. "Max... Max, as in Max my... dog?" Her eyes were wide with shock.

If possible, he grinned even wider at her.

The similarities between Max the man, and Max the dog were noticeable. When she saw the patch of white hair, it made her think of his white ear when he was an animal.

Her head fell into her hands. When she woke up, her migraine from earlier was gone, but another one was beginning after taking in this news. "Is this a prank? Is it

April Fool's and I don't know it? Why are you guys doing this? It's not funny." She was babbling, but she didn't care. "Maybe I'm just in a terrible dream and I haven't woken up yet." The last part she said to herself. She looked around the room. This was crazy. She had to get out of here. Without saying a word, she stood and headed to the front door.

Eli hurried to block her path. "This is a lot to process, Willow, but it's the truth."

She pushed past him and kept walking.

"Tell me about the man who has green eyes and has haunted your dreams since you were a child."

When Eli said the words to her back, it halted her trek. It was a few seconds before she turned and gaped at him. "How do you know that? I've never told anyone about him." Her suspicion was on high alert.

"Because your mother, Hyacinth, had the same nightmares... Killian was the man in your mother's dreams too."

To say it shocked her was an understatement. After her mother's death when she was nine, a family adopted her, and she moved to another state. Ever since then, she'd had no one who remembered her mother she could talk to or ask questions. The only things she had were a few pictures of the two of them together and her mom's old leather jacket. "You knew her?" Tears gathered in her eyes and threatened to spill.

"I met her once."

"I knew her." Zora stood. "You resemble her so much."

Tears trickled down Willow's face. This was someone that had met her mother. "Is my mom dead because she was an Oracle?" She looked to Eli for the answer.

No one said anything. They looked at her with sorrow and pity. She slunk back over to the sofa and dropped onto the cushions. Matty took her hand in hers.

"I want you to tell me everything. I need to know everything that concerns my life. That includes knowing more about this... Killian." Despite the tears, when she spoke, there was a steely resolve in her words that showed the depth of her inner strength.

"This is a bad idea." Morgan made sure they knew her opinion.

"I don't disagree with you, but the cat's out of the bag now." Zora sat next to Willow.

Eli took a seat on the coffee table in front of her. She fixed her eyes on him. He was the only one in the group that had not befriended her or talked to her. Curiosity ate at her insides, but she realized it was a conversation better left between them. "Tell me about Killian." She didn't care that it came out like she was issuing an order. They owed her the truth.

Phaedra, Max and Morgan found somewhere to sit while Eli began his story of Killian and his connection to her. They gathered around like they were listening to a ghost story being shared around a campfire.

"He's King of the Vampires and has been so for hundreds of years. A couple of years before your mother's death, he learned a family of Oracles existed."

"How..." Willow interrupted.

"We're still unsure how he came into the knowledge. There are different factions of supernaturals that are finding out this information." He returned to the tale.

Her mind couldn't stop thinking of the term, 'supernaturals,' that he'd used.

"You mean there's something more than witches, werewolves and vampires... and Oracles?" It was hard to keep the skepticism and sarcasm from her voice.

"Yes." Eli's response bordered on snarky. She looked him in the eyes and saw his annoyance with her tone. She didn't look away, and neither did he, but his gaze lost the irritation it held seconds ago. "Under Killian's reign, vampires haven't worked well with others."

Phaedra interrupted. "To clarify, he thinks vampires are the top of the food chain. Humans, supernaturals, we're all here as their endless blood supply."

Eli nodded and continued. "If a vampire is working with other supernaturals, it means they are an outcast. Other vampires won't hesitate to kill them. Think of it as being excommunicated."

"I thought vampires were immortal?"

Matty spoke. It was the first time since finding them here that Matty had talked. "There are powerful, black magic spells that can kill a vampire."

Her answer sounded ominous. None of the others spoke up to elaborate. Zora gave her a sharp look before she narrowed her eyes at her daughter. "We don't talk about that." The harshness in her tone startled Willow. She'd never heard Zora speak that way to Matty. Black magic or whatever it was appeared to be a touchy subject. The topic was better left alone.

Eli resumed. "Once Killian got a hold of the information about Oracles, he realized if he found the Oracle, he could either enslave and coerce them to tell him the futures they saw or make them a vampire. Then he would have their loyalty and obedience and he could use their abilities to control the future..."

"Which means he would always be steps ahead. He could manipulate the future and control everything and everyone: humans and the magical realm alike." Zora finished.

"Because of a vampire's telepathic ability, Killian could enter your mother's dreams."

"How?"

"We believe a witch helped him..."

Again, Willow interrupted him. "He's seen my face when he's invaded my dreams. In this day and age of social media and CCTV cameras, how has he not found me already?" The tremor in her voice told him she was barely holding her emotion and fear in check.

"We put up powerful spells of protection to keep him from learning your identity and lineage. Those things were accounted for... but I fear he may be closer to that information, especially if a witch is still helping him. I suspect that's why your migraine caused you to black out today. He's increasing his efforts to gain access to your mind so he can learn exactly who you are and where you might be."

Willow fell back against the sofa after hearing Eli's last statement.

"Since he already had a link to your mother, somehow he could connect with you. That's why you dream of him."

CHAPTER 4

Eli

IT WAS OBVIOUS Willow was struggling to digest the information. Fatigue was written on her face. "That's enough for today. Maybe you should rest."

He expected her to argue with him, so it surprised him when she nodded, got up and went back into his bedroom with everyone's eyes following her movements.

After she left, no one said a word. It was Matty, who broke the silence, giving voice to what everyone was thinking. "Who'll alert the Council she knows?" The room was silent again.

It was his responsibility. He should bear the Council's ire. "I will tell them the decision was mine when the time comes." Concern was etched on their faces. "It's fine. Whatever the consequences are I'll accept them." The situation was grave. Everyone's thoughts were on how he would have to answer for his disobedience. He couldn't dwell on that. There was a lot at stake. He could only hope the Elders would see reason before they meted out punishment.

"Right now we should make a plan. I fear that Killian may send out trackers. If a witch has betrayed us, we might not have much time before he knows that Willow is the Oracle."

More silence ensued. He was sure he'd have to convince them on why they needed to act when Phaedra spoke.

"She's not going to like it, but we have to move her."

He rewarded her with a small smile of thanks. "I agree. It's time for a road trip. We need to keep moving." Eli looked at the others to gauge their reactions.

"I assume you'll be the one to tell Willow she has to uproot her whole life. I think we know how well that will go over." Morgan gave him a saccharine sweet smile.

The short victory he'd celebrated over winning Phaedra to his side disappeared when he thought of the wrath Willow would unleash when he told her they had to leave Nashville.

Max clapped him on the shoulder. "Don't tell her the news when she's hangry." He shook his head over unpleasant memories of Willow's behavior when she was hungry and angry.

"Got it."

Zora stood. "Matty and I will get an RV, groceries and camping supplies."

Matty stood next to her mother with her arms folded across her chest. When Eli looked at her face, he saw a mixture of curiosity and annoyance over the question Phaedra asked Zora earlier and the embarrassment over being chastised for bringing up black magic. Both topics were sore spots for Zora. He didn't envy her that difficult conversation.

"Seven people on an RV. This should be cozy." No one reacted to Morgan's sarcasm.

"Willow takes the bedroom on the RV and the other sleeping space onboard, Mathilda can have. The rest of us will use tents or sleep under the stars." Eli issued orders. Most of the time he never tried to pull rank, but when they couldn't agree or he thought it would be a problem, he decided.

"Well now that that's settled I'm going home to pack and have a night of unhurried sex with my boyfriend." Phaedra grinned and pulled on Max's shirt.

He gave her a sly smile back and emitted a low growl. Heat and lust leapt between the two. The surrounding air crackled with sexual energy.

"On that note, everyone knows what needs to be done. Make sure you give a good enough reason on your jobs that won't leave anyone suspicious, raise questions or cause someone to send out a search party." He noticed they were going to use magic to leave his apartment and spoke up again. "Wait."

They stopped and looked at him.

"Until we're sure Killian isn't working with a witch, lets limit our magic. A decent witch can track magic. No teleporting. Use the human ways to travel."

They groaned at hearing this, everyone, but Max.

"We have to be cautious so we keep her safe."

No one argued further with his logic.

He let out a breath, after the group left. Everything had gone better than expected.

Something pulled him towards his bedroom. He stood outside the closed door for a few minutes before he opened it and peered inside the room. Willow lay on her side facing away from him. He assumed she must be asleep because she didn't stir. After closing the door, he headed into the kitchen. He wasn't the best cook without magic, but he didn't want her to wake up hungry. After what Max said, he didn't want to give her bad news on an empty stomach.

After he finished the meal he sat on the sofa and read through one of his incantation books. Studying the craft was always important to him. An impending battle was sure to come once Killian figured out she was the Oracle. He wanted them to be ready.

A few hours later, he was meditating when her voice interrupted the silence. "I know we have to leave."

Eli's eyes popped open, and he turned to look at her. They stared at one another.

There was nothing demure about Willow. She looked at you when she spoke to you. He didn't waver in his eye contact either. "Either you unintentionally overheard us talking, or you were eavesdropping?" He tried to mask the faint smile that played at the corner of his lips.

So much for the, 'I'm tired,' act she put on earlier.

"In my defense, I wasn't trying to be nosy. Your voices carry." She shrugged and walked further into the living room. A grin flashed across her face and then vanished in an instant.

"If you were going to listen to the conversation why didn't you stay out here?" He teased.

She ignored his quip. "I wanted to rest and think about everything, but then I fell asleep." She sat on the sofa and tucked one leg beneath her. From his position on the floor, he looked up at her. The way she chewed her bottom lip, told him she was pondering things, so he waited to let her speak. "It's weird that my dog knows so much about me. I do get a little scary when I'm hungry." She giggled, but then her expression turned gloomy and her shoulders slumped in realization. "I guess he's not my dog anymore." She let out a sigh.

He watched her face drop before she looked at her lap. The fact was her life was changing overnight. Often he saw her be brave and strong. Right now her vulnerability was shining through. Eli got up and sat next to her on the sofa. The thought of taking her hand in his was fleeting. "I know all this change isn't easy for you."

It was difficult not to be flustered by her proximity and the way she looked at him.

"In twenty-four..." He stumbled over his words and cleared his throat, "In less than twenty-four hours, you've had a ton of mind-blowing information dumped in your lap. Most people would have a rough time processing everything without it making them crazy. Yet you're intact and have your wits about you." He dropped his gaze. "I'm in awe of you."

The minute the words left his mouth he knew he shouldn't have said them. He stood and made to leave when she grabbed his arm. It was the first time she'd touched him and through his sleeve, the press of her hand felt as if it was trying to sear itself into his skin. He bit his lip to keep from letting a curse fall from his lips. In a few seconds, he composed his features into a mask and turned to look at her.

"Why didn't you speak to me that day?" Her eyes probed his for the truth.

The question startled him, but the day she referred to was hard to forget. He was unprepared to explain to her right now. Her eyes bore into his, trying to glean answers. Disconcerted, he swallowed and looked elsewhere. He spoke the first thought that came to mind. "You must be hungry."

She let her hand fall away at his words. He walked towards the kitchen and breathed a sigh of relief at having some space from her.

"I made dinner a couple hours ago, but I'll reheat it."

CHAPTER 5

Willow

IF SOMEONE HAD told her, she would have a conversation with her disdainful but attractive co-worker, while sitting in his apartment, she would have called them crazy. Yet, here she was.

Eli was a mystery. She had so many questions. One of which, he wasn't ready to answer. She watched him retreat into the kitchen. If she gave him more time, she hoped he'd tell her why he hadn't responded that day. She wanted to know why they'd never communicated like she had with the rest of the Protectors.

A couple minutes later, she followed him. Whatever he'd prepared smelled delicious. He moved around the kitchen unsure. She raised her eyebrows while she watched him. He caught the gesture and looked embarrassed. "Most of the time, I cheat and use magic so I can do something else. I haven't manually cooked in a while."

She looked at him wide-eyed, with her mouth gaped open. Even though he'd told her earlier they were witches, she still had a hard time believing it. "You cook with magic, like they do in Harry Potter? That's so cool. I know you told everyone not to use it, but just show me a little something. I won't tell." Awe and child-like wonder permeated her voice. "Cross my heart." She made the sign of the cross over her heart.

"You heard everything didn't you?" He quirked an eyebrow at her, daring her to lie.

She gave him a sheepish smile and looked away before she continued talking about magic, in the hopes he'd forget her listening to their conversation. "I would be the ultimate multi-tasker if I was a witch. Say 'Abracadabra' and make the food magically appear on the plate or something." Willow was giddy with excitement.

Eli chuckled. "I'm not a wizard. I don't say 'Abracadabra.'" He shook his head.

His explanation confused her. "What does that mean? I thought wizard was a name for a male witch."

He sighed and put down the pot he was holding. That comment appeared to get his undivided attention. "You watch too much television. First, regardless of gender, we're known as witches, those of us that practice white magic. Warlocks are witches that practice black magic. Wizards are charlatans, posers. They don't know magic, but are exceptional at trickery so they can give someone who doesn't know any better the illusion they do."

She digested the information he'd just given her.

"That's why everyone went silent earlier when Matty referenced black magic, because none of you practice it?"

He nodded and picked up the pot of noodles. "Yes. Now may I finish making dinner?"

"So you're not going to cook with magic?" She was expecting him to do tricks and wow her. Disappointment marred her brow, when he didn't whip out a magic wand or say a spell.

"You just said so yourself, that you overheard me tell everyone magic is off limits."

Her shoulders slumped in discontent and she pouted. "You can't do even a tiny little spell?"

"Nope."

She rolled her eyes. "Great. A witch who can't do any spells or magic."

Eli looked offended. "I didn't say I can't do magic. I'm just unable to do any at this time."

"Uh, huh."

He bristled at her disinterest and she had to hold back a sly grin. "Wizard." She mumbled under her breath, knowing it would get a rise out of him.

"I'm not a wizard! I can do magic!"

If she lit a match and threw it at him, he would have gone up in flames he was fuming so hard.

"Whatever." Maybe she'd just...

'STOP IT!'

The voice in her head was so loud and clear she nearly jumped out of her skin. Her head whipped from side to side, while her eyes scanned the room. She was going to ask Eli if he'd heard the voice too. When she looked at him she saw guilt written all over his face. It was the first time he wouldn't make eye contact with her. The shocking moment of clarity knocked her off her feet. It was his voice that spoke in her mind.

"How... how... how did..." She stuttered and tripped over her words while she stared at him and tried to make sense of what just happened.

"I'm sorry. I shouldn't have done that. It was an invasion." Eli wore a penitent expression. He still wouldn't look at her.

Her amazement was so strong her mouth dropped open in an, 'O' of surprise. She could not muster up the fury she was sure should course through her veins right now. "I thought you said you couldn't do magic?"

"That's not magic." He shook his head and continued to look contrite.

"The others can't do that. I'm the only one in our coven with telepathy." He looked at her. "I only enter someone's mind when I have permission. I promise I won't do that again." Eli returned to his dinner preparations.

After experiencing Eli's supernatural ability firsthand, she blurted out the question racing around her head. "Can you control people's minds?"

He sat the pot he was holding on the counter.

"I know I still owe you many explanations, but if it's okay, can we table this conversation for tomorrow. It's been a long day for me too."

They stared at one another. His eyes pleaded with her. She could force the issue and try to make him talk, but if she was honest, she wanted him to do it willingly, not because she was being a brat. She nodded. "Okay... so what's for dinner?"

For the first time, since she'd known him she saw a genuine smile light up his face. The guy was gorgeous before, but when he showed off the pearly whites, he took her breath away.

"It's an old family recipe for spaghetti and meatballs."

While the meal preoccupied him, she leaned on the counter and studied him. Eli had broad shoulders and was over six feet tall. Earlier he'd appeared awkward, but now he moved around the kitchen with the grace of a dancer. Underneath his clothes was a nice, chiseled, muscular physique.

At the office he wore dress shirts and dress pants. Today was no exception. He was a guy that didn't shy away from color. Today's shirt was lavender, and the slacks were a dark gray. She wondered what he looked like in something more relaxed, such as jeans. Her roaming gaze moved back up to his face. His azure blue eyes and dark hair made her think he could be the actor Henry Cavill's twin brother, because he had a Superman curl and a dimple on his chin.

Eli is sexy as hell.

She cleared her throat and stood up straighter. For the first time that day, she worried over her appearance. What had she put on this morning? She looked at her attire: black flats, black slacks and a basic white blouse. The clothing reminded her of the uniform a waiter wore at an upscale restaurant. Work clothes were so dowdy.

It could be worse.

Eli came to the end of his preparations.

What did it matter?

He wasn't the least bit interested in her. Now the once snobbish co-worker that never spoke to her, seemed to tolerate her because he had to protect her.

"Ready to eat?" His words broke her from her brooding. She gave him a smile she didn't quite feel.

"Yeah."

CHAPTER 6

Eli

THE RV ZORA bought looked like it was on its last legs. The older model motor home had seen better days. Paint was peeling in various places. There were a few rust spots near the bumper. Zora shrugged her shoulders at him when he gave her a look. "It was short notice. What did you expect?"

It wasn't so much the appearance of it he questioned, but the functionality. Was this heap of junk going to break down on them the minute they got on the road?

"Plus, you said you didn't want us using any magic... Say the word and this vehicle can look like it just rolled off the lot." Zora peered at him with a hopeful expression. When he didn't grant her permission to perform magic and transform the RV she stormed off.

The no magic policy was biting him in the ass. He needed to amend his rule. He beckoned Matty over to him. "Think you can find a counter spell to cover tracking spells?" He asked in a low voice.

"I'm on it." She smiled and went off to rummage in her backpack for one of the spell books she always carried.

No use in getting everyone's hopes up if they didn't find a powerful enough spell to keep their magic from being tracked.

He was testy after spending a restless night on his lumpy sofa with Willow fifty feet away in his bedroom. Besides lying awake, thinking of her all night, his long frame had barely fit comfortably.

After dinner, they'd both gone to bed, agreeing they needed to call it an early night. This morning, everyone had met them outside of her apartment. Phaedra, Max and Morgan were loading up the vehicle while they waited on Willow to finish whatever she was doing upstairs.

Eli glanced at his watch and then at the front door to her building for the fourth time in twenty minutes. He wanted to beat the early morning traffic, but that wasn't going to happen.

Maybe I should send someone in to get her.

As he peered at his watch once more, she emerged. She carried a large duffle bag, a guitar case and a backpack. Her still damp curls indicated she'd showered and changed clothes while she was upstairs. She wore a black, leather jacket over a band t-shirt and ripped up jeans. Her coily curls now sat on top of her head in a messy bun. "I'm surprised I didn't have you inside my brain telling me to hurry." She teased.

He rubbed at the back of his neck over the unease he felt and laughed. Max must have overheard her comment, because before he responded, Max blurted out, "So Eli told you he had telepathy and was a mind reader? Did he tell you about the people he coerced into forgetting your gigs..."

Phaedra elbowed him in the stomach trying to shush him, but the damage was already done. Willow's face crumpled. Everyone froze. His eyes locked on her, but in his periphery Max mouthed he was sorry.

"Is that true?" Her voice was just above a whisper. The betrayal erased the progress they'd made last night. "You all knew?"

They avoided the angry, accusatory glances she cast their way. The hurt she felt extended to everyone, not just Eli. "Why would you do that?" She directed the question at him.

Before he could respond, Willow balled up her fist and punched him.

"Ow!" The unexpected punch landed harder than he thought it would. He clutched at his eye for a minute, before he dropped his hand and squinted at her. He hadn't expected her to resort to violence.

"That's for the possible Grammy I missed out on," she punched him again in the same eye, "and that's for last night when you entered my mind without my permission."

"Ow!" He covered his eye once more. "Wait. Just stop okay." He held up his free hand in surrender, hoping she wouldn't hit him again. "Am I going to get any help here?" He looked towards the group, and they glanced away and pretended to be engaged in something else. "Do you think I enjoyed crushing your dream?"

Willow glared at him with her arms folded across her chest. She looked like she was ready to pummel him again. It was the tears gathered in the corners of her eyes that dissipated his anger at being punched. He had robbed her repeatedly of a music career and possible stardom. There were multiple producers and labels that were prepared to make her offers and he'd shut them all down, entered their thoughts and coerced them to change their minds and forget her. He'd taken no pleasure in it, but knew those words would fall on deaf ears. He told her the only thing he could. Hoping to ease some of her hurt and anger. "I had to do it to keep you safe. If you became famous, it would be easier for Killian to locate you. I..." He swallowed. "We couldn't let that happen... I'm sorry."

A lone tear slipped down her cheek and she swiped it away. She didn't say another word to him or anyone else. She picked up her bags and climbed up into the motor home. He heard the door leading to the sleeping area being slid shut.

He stood staring at the spot she'd just vacated. It was going to be a long road trip if she gave them the silent treatment the whole time. He only hoped, at some point she would understand and forgive him.

***

Phaedra drove the large vehicle expertly over the twisty, bumpy back roads. He hadn't wanted to take any chances traveling on well-known highways. They'd been on the road for two hours before she emerged from the bedroom.

Eli didn't turn around from the passenger seat when he heard the door slide open.

"Wanna play?" Matty's voice carried to the front of the cab.

"What are you guys playing?"

The vinyl bench of the dinette creaked when Willow took a seat.

He wanted to engage with her, but was certain what he'd done still upset her. Without looking over, he felt Phaedra glancing at him. "Eyes on the road." He didn't look over at her when he spoke.

"Boy, I was driving long before you were. I don't need you to tell me how to drive."

He sighed. The last person he wanted angry with him was Phaedra. She was the one that always had his back. "Sorry."

Neither of them said anything for minutes. The sounds of Morgan and Zora chattering about a magazine mingled with the laughter and slap of the cards coming from the dinette area where Max, Matty and Willow played a game.

"Why do you keep looking at me?"

"You know why." Phaedra fully turned her head to stare at his profile before she returned her eyes to the road. "Need I remind you she's off limits?"

Eli's face flushed and his eyes glittered with anger. He clenched his fist.

"What's all that bull you spouted off at Zora yesterday?"

"That's different and you know it. My relationship with Max is not forbidden."

Eli chewed on her words and let some of his indignation dissolve. She meant well. She didn't want to see him get hurt or suffer. "I know the Council's rules and the Protector's Commandment. I don't intend to disobey them. You don't need to worry about me." It was hard not to be angry. He turned and looked out the passenger window hoping the matter was now closed. The landscape of empty, overgrown fields and meadows passed by in a blur while he brooded.

CHAPTER 7

Willow

WILLOW WISHED SHE could hear what they were discussing. Phaedra and Eli must have been having a heated conversation if she was reading Eli's facial expressions correctly. Where she sat, her view of Phaedra was blocked.

Why can't I read lips or get in people's heads the way Eli can?

She laid down a card.

"What's wrong?" Matty played her turn, but looked at her with concern.

"Nothing." Willow pasted on a smile.

They continued playing the game. Even though she understood Eli's logic regarding her music career, her emotions were still raw over him keeping her from her dream. The irrationality of her feelings weren't lost on her,

43

but she couldn't help how she felt. It didn't stop her from wanting to get to know Eli. If she apologized for punching him, it might mend things between them.

"Isn't this dress cute, Morgana?"

Willow overheard Zora speaking. Even though she was in proximity to them, it felt like she was eavesdropping. Despite that, she intruded on the conversation.

"Um... I thought your name was Morgan? I get you guys have been lying to me for forever. Were your names not real either?" She tried to keep the irritation out of her voice. She wanted the betrayal to be water under the bridge, but the need to be spiteful was too good to pass up.

When she turned and looked at the two women they didn't seem the least bit remorseful for the secrecy and lies.

"Morgana is my given name. Morgan sounds less... witchy or magical." She chuckled.

Morgana's pixie haircut and the way she giggled reminded Willow of a fairy. If fairies existed in the supernatural world, Morgana could pass for Tinkerbell. Willow smiled at her.

"My name is Zoriana Walker." She closed the magazine she'd been reading.

"Zoriana, Zora, they are both beautiful names."

"Thank you."

Willow swiveled around and glanced at Matty. "What's your full name?"

"Mathilda." She motioned towards the front of the motor home. "You know Phaedra. She prefers her given name. No nicknames for her, at least not to her face." Her voice dropped to a whisper during the last part and she smirked. When she spoke again, she returned to a normal tone. "Eli is short for Elias. Everyone calls him Eli except for Phaedra. She's the only one allowed to call him by his first name."

"Why is that?"

"It's just the way it is." Mathilda shrugged.

"We're all Walkers. Related either by blood or marriage." Zoriana offered.

Willow was okay with learning everyone's names for now. She wasn't ready to decipher or unravel the family tree that connected all of them.

Max is a werewolf though. Is he a Walker?

"But you're not a Walker, right?" She directed the question at Max.

"Nope! My full name is Gou Maximilian Okami. You can still call me Max."

It was impolite to stare, but every time she looked at him she saw her dog. She missed him.

Max must have sensed her melancholy. He let out a small whine reminiscent of one he often did in dog form and smiled at her.

I guess he could sense my moods.

For the next few hours, they continued to ride the country roads until Eli decided it was time for them to make camp. Phaedra drove the RV through the brush and they came to a peaceful looking clearing.

Everyone got out of the vehicle and stretched their limbs before they unloaded tents, sleeping bags and other camping gear. Max gathered wood to build a fire.

Willow half expected him to run into the woods in his wolf form and bring back a rabbit or some other small forest creature for dinner. Unlike her fantasy, Max returned on his human legs carrying bundles of branches and twigs. Then, without a single match, gasoline or rubbing two sticks together Morgana came and spoke one word over the pile. "Ignis." The wood burst into flames in seconds.

Color me impressed.

Why hadn't Eli done something similar when she asked him to do magic?

"What did I say about no magic?" Eli sported an annoyed look, like a teacher scolding a student that wasn't paying attention, when he lectured her.

"Sorry." She gave him an unapologetic shrug and winked at Willow.

For dinner, Zoriana pulled store-bought fish from the refrigerator inside the RV, and cooked the meal over the open flame using a skillet. So much for the fantasy that played in her head.

In her twenty-six years, she'd never been camping out in the woods. She didn't count spending the night in your backyard as a kid. Once night fell, the sky was riddled with thousands of stars that burned bright. After she ate, she stretched out on a blanket to stare up at them. Eli had given her a wide berth ever since they stopped and made camp. She decided she'd save her apology for another day. Let him sweat a little longer.

Before she knew it, she'd fallen asleep. It wasn't long before the vampire king entered her dream. She was back in his throne room, but this time he was standing instead of sitting. He was closer, much closer.

"Killian." She murmured. Before she spoke again, she saw movement out of the corner of her eye and realized they weren't alone. A statuesque bombshell, of Middle Eastern descent, stood a few feet behind him. Her golden brown eyes glowed with fiendish glee. Red lipstick painted her lips and reminded Willow of blood. The tight, black leather suit she wore looked like a second skin. She was a video game character come to life, the epitome of a thirteen-year-old boy's fantasy of a hot woman who could kick butt.

Willow tore her eyes away from the drop-dead gorgeous, but lethal looking woman and put her attention back on him. Her fear was so palpable her body quaked with it. He noticed. It was an aphrodisiac to him. He bathed in her terror. "Willow, I was wondering when we would see each other again." His long strides had him standing in front of her in a mere second. His voice was akin to icy tentacles running up and down her spine.

She was trying hard to push her panic to the side. Eli mentioned they thought a witch was helping him. Was that woman the witch? Maybe he would tell her.

"How did you find out my name?" A little confidence engulfed her, when her voice didn't shake when she spoke.

Killian shook his head and smirked. "You do not get to ask questions."

He advanced upon her again and stupidly she wished she were Dorothy from the *Wizard of Oz* and could click her heels together and go home.

Wake up.

She wished she was in her own bed with Max the dog, without the knowledge of any supernaturals, her lineage or why Killian wanted her.

Tears were leaking out of the corners of her eyes, but she dared not reach up and wipe them away.

What can he do to me in a dream?

She wasn't sure if he read her thoughts or if he'd always been planning to touch her. Before she could blink or have another thought, he seized her head between his hands. In an instant, the fiercest pain imaginable gripped her. Her eyes rolled back in her skull. A fever that made her skin tingle like it was being licked by millions of tiny flames consumed her whole body. An ocean roared in her ears.

"Tell me what I want to know. Who are you? What is your last name? Where are you?"

She did the only thing she could do. The agonizing scream that ripped itself from her throat sounded otherworldly even to her.

Everlasting pain tore through her until seconds later she saw the stars again. The hellish torment ceased and then she heard Eli. "Willow! Willow!" His voice was authoritative and demanding, but it didn't mask the fear vibrating in his body while he held her.

She only knew it for what it was because she shook with it too. Her gaze drifted up to his face. "Eli?" She was so glad to see him. In his arms she felt safe, like nothing bad could ever touch her again.

Once her fear subsided, she noticed that everyone crowded around them. Their faces didn't hide their panic. Zoriana was holding her hand.

"It... it was... it was Killian." She had to force the words past her lips. "He..." She gulped and struggled to breathe. "He... he knows my name." She registered their shock after she spoke.

Eli held her tighter.

"His hands... tou... touched me and my body... it was on fire." She tilted her head back and looked at Eli's face. His grave expression scared her. Things were more serious than she realized. She calmed herself enough to get the next words out without stuttering.

"He was trying to force me to tell him who I am and where I am."

Someone gasped, but she wasn't sure who made the sound. Her gaze was locked on Eli.

CHAPTER 8

Eli

THE FEAR THAT seized his insides only increased the more Willow divulged her dream. He'd never wanted to be right about Killian getting closer, but her nightmare confirmed it. "You're safe now." He rocked her in his arms until the tremor left her body. "We push on from here bright and early tomorrow."

He didn't want her asking questions or being fearful anymore tonight so he communicated through his mind link to the others.

'HER TRAINING NEEDS TO BEGIN AT ONCE.' He looked at Zoriana before he told them the next thing. 'PLUS, WE HAVE TO PAY SAMSON A VISIT.'

'NO.' Zoriana's eyes skittered away from Mathilda when she responded.

'IT'S A NECESSITY.' His tone brooked no room for argument.

Zoriana gave him a dirty look before she left the group in a huff. The others each made a subtle nod and moved off to seek their beds.

By the time, he carried Willow into the RV Mathilda had crawled up to the overhead sleeping space above the cab. He placed her on the bed and went to walk away.

"Please stay with me tonight." Her voice was soft.

Eli turned. He was in awe of her again. The dream must have been excruciating for her, but she shed no tears.

"I'm afraid to go back to sleep right now..." Her eyes pleaded with him.

"Just until you fall asleep." He lay on the bed beside her with his hands folded together over his stomach and stared up at the ceiling. For several minutes, neither of them said a word.

"Next time Killian enters your dream, punch him. That will keep him away... my eye still smarts a little." He smiled and touched the corner of his eye.

Willow snorted then chuckled. "I wish I could say I'm sorry." She chuckled some more before she sobered.

"It's okay."

She twisted on her side and faced him. "I didn't know you were such a joker."

Even though he wasn't looking at her, he saw her smile out of the corner of his eye.

"I have my moments. Thought you could use a laugh." He turned and glanced at her. She no longer seemed scared. Her eyes were warm and inviting. This was a mistake. He shouldn't be in here, lying next to her. His gaze shifted back to the ceiling.

Maybe I should leave.

"Would you tell me about my mother?" The request came out on a breathless whisper, like she'd been working up the nerve to ask the favor of him.

He took a second to find his voice. "You were nine when she died?"

She nodded. "Yes... I remember her, but sometimes she fades. It would help to hear someone else's memories of her."

He turned to face her. "I only saw her the one time." He was afraid to disappoint her. If only he had a thousand moments of her mother he could share.

"It's okay. I'd rather have that one memory than nothing at all."

He squinted his eyes and licked his bottom lip as his mind dredged up his encounter with her mom.

"I was twelve when she visited. She had hair just like yours..." He looked at Willow and she smiled and ran her hand over her curls. "Non-witches aren't normally invited into the coven. Protectors brought her, because she found out who they were. They had no choice. She was jumpy and frightened. No one knew why." He was unsure if he should continue. He hadn't thought about these memories for a long time and now that he'd remembered them, he wasn't sure he should share. "This isn't a good idea." He was going to sit up, when she tugged on his arm.

"Please."

He made the mistake of looking into her eyes again and he knew he wouldn't refuse her. He pushed his back against the headboard and stared at the wall of the motor home.

"They took her to the Council's chamber where the Elders convene. I shouldn't have been there, but I snuck inside the room. I hid in the corner and listened to her talk of things she'd seen. Events that hadn't happened yet." He relived the memory as he spoke.

He dreaded the next thing he would say. "Your mother spoke of her own death. She'd seen it." Willow sat up. He chose not to look at her. "At that point, the Elders began to talk over one another. In the middle of the chaos, she saw me. When she spoke again, everyone fell silent. She saw me and gave me the kindest smile. Then she told me someday I would be one of your Protectors. The shouting started all over again when they realized I was in the room and they had me removed before they let her continue."

"What else did she tell them?"

When he looked in her eager eyes, he wished again that he had more to give her, even if they were only crumbs.

"They never shared it with me." He wondered what else they said as well. "We should rest. We need to get an early start tomorrow."

Willow lay back down. "You'll stay until I fall asleep?"

"Yes."

When she shut her eyes, he tried not to watch her. She was beautiful. He hated this pull he felt towards her. He tore his gaze away and settled for the view of the wall.

Thirty minutes later, she'd fallen asleep. The thought of her waking violently in the middle of the night kept him rooted to the bed.

What if she needs me?

He would stay here tonight. Just in case. He made himself comfortable propped against the headboard and closed his eyes.

The next morning, someone poked him in the chest. He awoke to find Phaedra standing over him with a look of displeasure. Under her harsh gaze, he felt like a young boy being reprimanded by his mother. He looked at Willow and noticed she still slept. He got up from the bed and left the RV with her close on his heels. Before he spoke, he made sure they were a safe distance away so they wouldn't be overheard. "Listen, I know what it looked like."

Phaedra crossed her arms over her chest and gave him a scowl he knew all too well.

"She was afraid to sleep alone. That's why I stayed. You were there. You saw the nightmare she had."

The hostility left Phaedra's body. "I'm worried that soon you won't be able to draw the line."

He looked away and ran his hand over his face.

"You have feelings for her, Elias."

He glared at her with clenched fists. "That doesn't mean I will act on them. I know the oath I made. You don't have to keep reminding me." He bit his lip to avoid speaking out of anger.

Phaedra's eyes roamed over his face. He dropped his gaze to the ground, not wanting to meet her discerning look.

"You are like a brother to me... I just don't want to see this end badly." She squeezed his shoulder. "C'mon. We need to wake everyone else and get moving."

He nodded, and they walked side-by-side back to camp.

Once everybody was up Zoriana passed around protein bars and they packed everything into the RV and hit the road.

Max was behind the wheel this time with Phaedra riding shotgun. He sat on the sofa next to Morgana reading an incantation book and trying his best to feel unaffected by Willow. She was cross-legged on the bed with the door open, plucking at the strings of her guitar and humming. Even though she sang no words, the spell she cast over him with the melody from the instrument and her crooning threatened to shatter his resolve. He tried to refocus on the page he'd reread over and over.

Zoriana still wasn't talking to him, which was to be expected. He wished she was speaking to him, so he could engage her in conversation and drown out the sound of Willow's voice. With everything that was going on, he couldn't afford to be at odds with Zoriana. He would have a talk with her later. Visiting Samson was anathema to her, but was necessary.

CHAPTER 9

Willow

"WHERE ARE WE?" She jumped off the step of the motor home. Her boots landed in muddy water and she grimaced.

The old warehouse was in an industrial part of town among a bunch of identical, dilapidated warehouses. Before she could get an answer to her question, a burly man emerged from the building. A few armed men flanked him. Unlike them, he carried no weapons she could see.

His dark, bald, head gleamed and from the distance she was at she could make out the tattoos that marked his scalp. The top part of his grayish-blue coveralls was rolled to his waist exposing bulging biceps and forearms that were also covered in tattoos. The wife beater he wore was tinged with grime and what looked to be motor oil.

"What do you want?" His deep baritone rattled her. Why were they here? What did they want from this guy? Danger surrounded him.

"Is that how you treat old friends?" Eli stepped out of the RV and walked towards him.

The scowl never left the man's face as he watched him approach. Eli stopped a foot in front of him. Willow watched the staredown with butterflies flapping in her stomach. A smile crept across the man's face and then he shouted a whoop of joy and grabbed him in a hug. Eli's feet left the ground when he was hefted into the air.

"My man!"

"It's good to see you too, Samson. Can you put me down?" Eli chuckled.

When she looked around she saw Phaedra, Max and Morgana grin and walk towards Eli and Samson. Zoriana hung back. Mathilda watched her mother and when Zoriana took a step forward so did she. Willow brought up the rear. By the time she caught up with the group, everyone was headed inside the building.

The interior of the space resembled a chop shop. Rows of cars lined the room and were in various phases of disassembly. A few mechanics worked on vehicles. The men that had accompanied Samson out to greet them still clutched their weapons while they walked.

What are we doing here?

In answer to her thought, Samson pulled a lever that looked like a switch on an electrical box. After he flipped it, the wall moved to the side. It opened enough so they could file through one at a time. Motion sensor lights cut on inside the cavernous room to reveal tons of guns, ammo, machinery, vehicles and other weaponry, some of which she'd never seen before.

"What are you in need of?" Samson raised his arms and motioned around the warehouse.

Samson was looking at them when his gaze landed on Zoriana. His expression changed to one of shock, as if he'd seen a ghost. She looked elsewhere. The exchange wasn't lost on Eli. He coughed. "Lets walk around and have a look. That okay?"

Samson nodded still wearing a stunned look. Willow was eager to hang back and figure out what the story was between Samson and Zoriana when Max took her arm and dragged her away. Morgana steered Mathilda in another direction.

"Hey!" She tried to tear her arm out of Max's grasp.

"Give them their privacy. If you were in her position you wouldn't want an audience either." His disappointment came through in his words, but he let her go and left the decision to her.

She looked at the floor in shame. "Sorry." She mumbled and followed Max through the rows of knives, swords and battleaxes. It was endless. Her eyes were drawn to a small dagger with a jeweled hilt. There was no one to stop her so she took it off the wall and flipped it over in her hands. She pulled it from the brown leather scabbard and examined it. The metal gleamed in the faint light. She could see her reflection. When she glanced up, Max was at the end of the aisle, about to turn. She pushed the blade back into the sheath and slipped it through her belt loop before she ran to catch up with him.

Once she rounded the corner behind him, she found everyone save Zoriana and Samson looking over unique weapons. She stood beside Eli so she could see what held his attention. "What is it?" Her eyes scanned the weapon that looked more like a prototype for a futuristic gun.

Eli opened his mouth to answer her when Samson's big voice rang out in answer.

"I call that my Vervain Launcher," After he walked over, his fingers caressed the gun with reverence, "You can use garlic in it if you were in a pinch and didn't have vervain. Both are Kryptonite to a vampire. And this is my Holy Water Gun." He indicated the weapon that lay near it that looked identical to a flame-thrower.

"So vervain is a thing? It works on vampires?" Despite everything she'd learned and seen so far, it always fascinated her when something else she only thought was myth turned out to be true.

"Yep. Vervain is also known as verbena or herb-of-the-cross. Ancient Romans, Persians and Celtic druids believed it was sacred and used it to ward off evil and sometimes for religious rites." He stepped closer and held her gaze, keeping her enthralled. "It was even believed to have been used to stop Jesus' wounds from bleeding after they pulled him from the cross." Once he walked away, the spell he'd cast with his story, broke. He continued his explanation. "Which is why people used it to keep vampires away. Add it to a charm, put it in a drink or place it near you and it should protect you from the bloodsuckers."

Samson knew a lot about this stuff. What kind of supernatural hunted other supernaturals? "Are you a witch, a shapeshifter or something?"

Samson guffawed. "Nope. Just a human."

"So humans know about supernaturals? Are there many of you?" It fascinated Willow.

Samson's face soured. "Most humans are blissfully unaware of the existence of supernaturals and only consider them fairy tales and myths. Not all humans are as accepting as me. It scares many of the ones that have the knowledge of magic. They're distrusting which resulted in them creating zealot and conspiracy theorist militias."

"That doesn't stop you from selling your weapons to any of these crazies looking to kill us." Max fumed and took a threatening step towards Samson.

"I'm open for business to everyone." Samson didn't back down from his challenge as the men squared off against one another.

"You might not want to get too close to that." With the arch of his brow and a nod he indicated what was behind Max. "That's pure, undiluted silver. I know you werewolves have an allergic reaction to silver more so than vampires."

Max's head jerked around to look behind him. Hanging on the wall was a large silver net that looked as thin as a spider's web. He backed away with a low snarl.

"Hey! We're here as friends remember?" Eli stepped in between the two men ready to fight each other.

Phaedra touched Max on the arm and he stepped back.

Eli glanced at Max, who was shaking with fury. "One of our commandments state that a Protector shall always have his comrades back. That weapon could harm Max. We'd never buy a weapon that could harm one of our own." Max's anger drained away at his words. He nodded in thanks. Eli turned back to Samson. "Can you show us some other toys you have lying around?"

Samson gave Max the stink eye once more before he led Eli to another part of the room.

Willow was in awe of the way Eli diffused the situation and wondered what else the Protector's Commandment stated.

As she followed everyone to another area of the warehouse, Samson's account of the human factions that opposed the supernaturals intrigued her. Once the thoughts drifted away she perused the walls and tables of weaponry. Occasionally, she picked up an item and inspected it, still unsure what most of the equipment was used for or who it was used to hurt.

"You planning to pay for that?" Samson's voice was low. She didn't have to turn around to know he was right at her back.

"I wasn't going to steal it if that's what you mean," She ran her finger across the dagger she'd stuck in her belt loop a while ago. "I just forgot it was there." She peered at the blade and then at Samson in defiance.

"Add it to the bill."

Willow looked up and caught Eli watching her. She mouthed 'thank you.' Without responding, he turned away from her and headed in another direction. He seemed upset.

Did he think I was planning to steal?

The indignation over how little he thought of her after last night made her place the dagger on the table. She walked away, but halted. Some part of her didn't want to leave it behind. A quick glance back almost had her giving in, but she cursed under her breath when her stubborn pride had her leaving empty-handed instead of retrieving the blade.

Twenty minutes later, they carried various packages to the motor home. Zoriana was the last to board after saying a private goodbye to Samson. She bit her tongue so she wouldn't ask Zoriana about her relationship with him. Mathilda wasn't the only one that had questions. Instead, she asked a question that wouldn't get her into trouble. "If you're witches, what do you need with these weapons?" She poked at a parcel sitting on the table in front of her.

Eli, who was now riding shotgun, turned to answer. "Yes, we have magic, but every bit helps. If we're kept from doing magic, those weapons will come in handy. Better to be over prepared." He turned his eyes back to the road and left her to her thoughts.

The vehicle ate up the miles and as the sky darkened to inky black, Eli allowed Phaedra to guide the RV down a dirt roadway that came to a dead end at a clearing much like the one they'd slept in the night before.

Again, she got the cold shoulder from him while everyone worked to get the camp set up and the fire started. The changes in his mood were making her head spin. She had enough on her mind without worrying about how he felt towards her. Once she ate dinner she went to bed, hoping she wouldn't encounter Killian, who haunted her dreams or need Eli, who now haunted her waking hours.

CHAPTER 10

Eli

THE NIGHT PASSED with no shrieks from Willow piercing the quiet. As he sipped his coffee, he hoped she'd gotten a good night's sleep. It was early in the morning and he intended to use every bit of daylight possible to begin her training. He planned on them being here for several days so she could train. "Okay everyone, I'm getting ready to make your day." He smiled at them. "We're using our powers again."

Morgana pumped her fist in the air. Zoriana and Mathilda high-fived. They weren't the only ones that felt hindered by not having magic.

"Now that we have to be on high-alert for Killian or his minions we need magic. I want everyone of you studying whenever you have a free minute. We have to learn spells that will help us in the fight against the vampires."

"Why don't we study some black magic spells that kill them?" Mathilda asked innocently and stood from where they'd been squatting next to the fire.

A hush fell over everyone. In a flash, Zoriana stood and smacked her daughter hard across the face. Everybody looked aghast. "Never ask about black magic again." The harsh resoluteness of Zoriana's voice kept Eli from chiding her. The older Protectors knew and understood the dangers of even the curiosity of black magic, let alone the practice of it, but Mathilda was so young. Sometimes he forgot she was only seventeen and hadn't bared witness to some of its atrocities. She'd been one of the youngest Protector recruits in its history and was still learning.

"Go wake up, Willow." He hoped giving her the chore gave her time to regain her composure. That kind of embarrassment in front of her peers more than likely stung her pride.

It was hard not to coddle her. If he did, he'd only be pouring salt on the open wound. She didn't want to be treated like a child.

Clutching her cheek and fighting back her tears, she stomped off to do as she was told, slamming the door to the RV after she entered.

Morgana was about to rebuke Zoriana, but Eli shook his head at her to leave it alone. She snapped her mouth closed and looked at him with insolent eyes.

"We have a cloaking spell to do. Let's get to it." Putting everyone to work might alter the sour mood that had taken root.

"Et pallium, quo praesidio perimetri." At the edge of camp, he chanted while he pointed his palms outward to set the spell.

While Mathilda was in the RV soothing her wounded pride and trying to rouse Willow from her slumber, the rest of them walked the perimeter casting various cloaking spells to keep their whereabouts hidden.

***

The coffee had grown cold by the time she emerged from the motor home. Sleep traced lines across her face. She rubbed her eyes and staggered towards the fire. It didn't go unnoticed that Mathilda wasn't with her.

"Is there any coffee?" She looked around for another mug.

"It's cold now." He poured the dregs from his cup onto the ground. "You can get some later. Right now, it's time for your training." He stood and pulled an object from the back of his waistband and tossed it at her.

Caught by surprise, she fumbled with the dagger she'd left behind at Samson's before the sheathed blade settled in her hands.

"I put this back." She looked at him with wide-eyed confusion.

"And I got it." He walked away, lest she ask more questions and want to know why he retrieved it. "It suits you." It was the only response he would give her. He turned towards her and took multiple steps backwards while he spoke. "Charge me."

"What?" Her voice squeaked out. She looked from him to the knife.

"I said, 'Charge me.'" He stood in front of her several feet away.

She still seemed unsure, so he used reverse psychology on her.

"Just as well. I figured you didn't have it in you. I must tell Phaedra she owes me ten dollars." He lied knowing the last detail of a supposed bet against her would rouse her anger.

The second he finished, she roared and charged at him. It was hard not to show amusement as she ran towards him with the now unsheathed dagger outstretched in her hand, intent on injuring him. Before she could strike he disappeared and then reappeared behind her.

Her head whipped back and forth, looking for him. He cleared his throat, and she whirled around to face him. "No fair. How am I supposed to fight with you when you're using magic?" She pouted and her shoulders slumped in defeat. "I thought you guys weren't doing magic right now. Something about it being tracked?"

He smirked. "We resumed this morning."

She flipped him the middle finger, and he doubled over in laughter. After a minute, he sobered. "I was showing you the magic you so craved the other night, but playtime is over." He walked towards her. "The war that's coming won't be fair. Killian won't fight fair. You will battle those that have magic or you might have to fight in hand-to-hand combat. We'll start out by teaching you how to defend yourself and how to use smart tactics to attack your opponent. It's not always brute strength that wins, but a cunning mind." He touched his temple with his pointer and middle fingers. "Max, Phaedra and I will train you each day and then Zoriana and Morgana will help you unleash your Oracle power." By the time he finished talking he stood an arm's length away from her.

Willow looked over at Max and Phaedra. Max cracked his knuckles. Phaedra held two staves in her hand and appeared ready to go into gladiator mode. She didn't intend to hold back, and that's exactly what he wanted. They didn't have much time and couldn't afford to take it easy on her. Willow might hate him by the end of this, but one thing was certain, she would be ready to face Killian and anyone else that came for her.

"Phaedra will give you your first lesson."

She tossed a staff to Willow, who missed it. The large stick hit the ground with a thud. She peeked at Phaedra with a sheepish expression painting her face. Phaedra wore a blank look. She picked up the staff and crouched low in a fighter's stance.

"Rush her." He called out to Willow.

She gaped at him unsure.

He nodded. "Yes, you. Rush her."

She glanced back at Phaedra and then ran as if her life depended on it, which it somewhat did.

Phaedra knocked her to the ground easily, exerting no energy. After falling, the weapon dropped out of her hands. The hard fall knocked the wind out of her. Phaedra picked up the staff and then reached out a hand to a groaning Willow, who clutched her stomach. She looked at Phaedra's outstretched hand and reluctantly accepted it. Her frustration and anger at being bested presented itself in her pursed lips, furrowed brow and rapid rise and fall of her chest. She dusted herself off and snatched her stick back.

"Don't fight angry. You won't win against her." Eli tried to offer the much-needed advice, but it was clear his words were going in one ear and out the other. It was obvious she hated to lose.

A repeat of the same incident happened several more times. She charged. Phaedra knocked her to the ground. Willow got up angry and repeated the same action again, and again and again.

"They say the definition of insanity is doing the same thing repeatedly and expecting a different result." If he said the words before her eighth attempt, would she heed his warning?

Nope.

As she lay on her back yet again, he approached her and stood over her. She was panting and perspiring, whereas Phaedra hadn't so much as broken a sweat.

"Are you going to listen? Or do you prefer to keep doing the same thing and getting the same result? Anger will not defeat Killian."

Those words appeared to reach her. She nodded and let him help her to her feet. Now that she'd worked that out of her system the three of them walked her through the basics of combat. The training lasted until the middle of the afternoon when they broke for lunch.

When they joined the others around the fire, Zoriana and Mathilda still weren't speaking to each other. Poor Morgana looked happy to see them.

"What's for lunch?" Willow dropped to the ground exhausted.

Zoriana passed her a plate and without waiting for an answer she wolfed down the food.

They had worked her hard so far and the day wasn't even over.

Eli lay back in the cool grass.

'ARE YOU GOING TO EAT?'

He bolted into a sitting position and gawked at Willow. No one noticed the change in his demeanor. They continued to chatter, chomp and munch around them.

'HOW DID YOU DO THAT? I USUALLY HAVE TO INITIATE THE CONVERSATION IN SOMEONE'S MIND.'

A surprised look passed over her face and her eyebrows shot up into her hairline. 'I DON'T KNOW. I JUST DID... YOU MEAN THIS ISN'T NORMAL?'

'YOU STARTING A CONVERSATION IN MY HEAD? NO.'

"You okay?" Mathilda asked and offered him a plate. Absently, he took it. He couldn't have told you what he was eating. Everything he put in his mouth was tasteless as he thought about what just happened.

Is she telepathic too?

Often throughout the meal, he stared at her. Since the Oracle was usually unaware of her abilities, what if she was capable of far more than they knew?

When he glanced at Willow, she seemed to be in quiet reflection. Tomorrow, they would forgo combat training to test her Oracle capabilities.

CHAPTER 11

Willow

THE NEXT MORNING it surprised her when instead of handing her a weapon to begin combat training, Eli took her to a quiet area of the meadow. He sat in front of her cross-legged. Morgana and Zoriana were nearby in the same position.

"Close your eyes and take deep breaths." He demonstrated the technique he wanted her to use.

She shut her eyes and followed his instructions.

"Okay, good job. Now keep your eyes closed and let everything fall away. Don't think about yesterday, today or tomorrow. Just clear your mind. Make it as blank as you can."

She squeezed her eyes shut and concentrated on what he wanted her to do. The more she tried to empty her mind, the more it was flooded with things that happened in the past and everything going on with her current situation. How the hell was she supposed to do this? Try as she might, she was unable to do what he asked. She would open her eyes and tell him so.

"Deep breaths. Stay calm and allow it to happen. Don't overthink it."

Annoyance sprang up inside of her.

Deep breaths my ass!

She shoved herself to her feet and stomped away. Eli was close on her heels. "Where are you going?"

"I'm not doing this. Why aren't we doing combat training?" She kept walking.

"Because this is more important. We need to help you develop your power as the Oracle and see if you have other gifts."

She shook her head. "This is stupid." Her nostrils flared.

"You're only saying it's foolish because you're having a hard time with it."

She didn't respond, but kept walking away, although at this point she had no idea if she was heading in the right direction. It was easy for him; he had magic. She huffed. Eli stopped following her. "I never figured you for a quitter." He called out.

Her footsteps halted. He always used logic that made her stop? She hated when he was right. Stomping her foot, she turned to face him.

'YOU'RE AN ASSHOLE.'

The big smirk he wore in victory was infuriating.

***

Over the past several days, they'd alternated between combat training in the mornings and what she called Oracle training. It often seemed like she was cramming for an exam she knew she would never pass. She was doomed to fail. There was a good possibility she would never get this. Every time she came to the meadow for this training her steps lagged because she felt defeated. Shouldn't she be able see the future by now? Was she the only Oracle in history that hadn't been capable of manifesting her powers?

She plopped down on the ground. "Why do I have to do this? I suck." She folded her arms across her chest.

He sat opposite her.

"It's because you're trying to force it. It needs to happen organically. Today we'll try a new approach."

Eli bent his legs into the cross-legged position and shut his eyes. "Close your eyes."

She gave him a look overflowing with skepticism, but shut her eyes.

"I realized that part of your problem is that you don't know how to meditate. You need to learn that before we dive into the heavy stuff."

Cracking one eye open, she peered at him. Today, just the two of them were in the meadow. At the realization she was out here alone with Eli her body temperature rose a few degrees. Even though he still dressed like a professor, it didn't take away from how sexy she found him: Eli, the sexy, magical professor. Her panties grew wet at the fantasies her mind conjured. The setting was intimate: an overgrown field of wildflowers, a beautiful sunny day and privacy. The only thing missing was —

"Close your eyes."

She shut her eyes at once.

How the hell did he know they were open?

Then another thought occurred.

Oh, my God. I hope he wasn't reading my thoughts.

Her face flushed, but she kept her eyes closed in case he now had his eyes open. She resumed the deep breathing to help slow her racing heart.

"Remember, deep breaths." He illustrated by inhaling and exhaling slowly.

She mimicked his breathing pattern. Over twenty minutes into meditating, something happened. Images in her head drifted away. Every event that led to this moment disappeared. Even the thoughts she'd had of tomorrow vanished. Soon the only thing she saw in her head was white space. It was bizarre to have her mind cleared of everything. The sensation didn't last for long. A flood of visions passed through. An inner voice told her the things she was seeing hadn't yet taken place. She saw the future, but it was passing in such quick succession she couldn't get a sense of what it was or what it meant.

Far off she could hear Eli calling her name. Once his voice broke through, she began to lose focus and the images shut off. She opened her eyes and blinked several times.

"I've been calling you for a while."

She gaped at him. "I saw something, but I don't understand what I saw ... it flashed by in a blur."

He grabbed her by the shoulders. "What?" His face broke out in a huge grin. The biggest grin she'd seen on him to date. "What did you just say?"

She giggled. "You heard me... it worked."

He threw his arms around her and they rolled over into the grass. "This is great. You did it."

She looked up at him. He'd never done that: initiated contact with her. Often, it seemed like he went out of his way to not touch her.

"Yeah... we did it. I couldn't have accomplished it without you."

Something in her words sparked some sort of awareness in him, because he removed his body from hers. "I'm sorry." He stood and wiped the bits of grass and twigs from his pants.

She sat up. "It's okay." She reassured him. It was hard not to feel confused. One minute they were laughing and the next he was treating her like she was a leper. Did he find her that repulsive that he always needed to get away from her?

"That's enough for today. We'll resume tomorrow." Eli rushed off without looking in her direction.

She plucked a clump of grass and threw it in frustration. "Ahhhhh!" She yelled at the sky before she dropped back into the grass. Why did she have to have feelings for her snobbish, magical co-worker who wasn't interested in her? She couldn't even enjoy the fact she'd just glimpsed the future. In a tantrum, she kicked her heel and banged her fist against the ground. Why did life seem so unfair?

Why do men get to have everything?

For women it's always one or the other. You can have a great career, but no family. Guess it worked that way in the magical realm too. Powers, but you're single.

CHAPTER 12

Eli

AFTER HE LEFT Willow, he ventured off into the woods. The joy they both felt over her power presenting itself almost caused him to kiss her. He never should have been alone with her. He was playing with fire. If he wasn't careful, forget about being burned, he would be incinerated.

In his anger, he hurled a fireball at a nearby shrub. It dissolved to black ash and drifted to the ground.

The rest of the day, he stayed out in the woods gathering herbs and practicing spells and incantations.

When he returned in the evening, everyone was sitting around the campfire talking and laughing. He noticed that after two weeks, Zoriana and Mathilda still weren't speaking. They sat as far away from one another as they could. Between Zoriana's jaded, unknown past and the slap, Mathilda was dealing with a lot. He needed to rectify the situation tomorrow. Zoriana had secrets, and was entitled to them, but their feud had gone on long enough.

"We were wondering when you'd return?" Mathilda smiled at him when he sat next to her.

"I'm here now cousin." He gave her a playful nudge and redirected his attention to the others.

"Help us, Eli. I was just telling Willow here that Phaedra thinks she's an amazing singer. Of course I've heard her sing because I used to be her pet, but you, Zoriana and Mathilda haven't. We're sitting around a campfire, there should be music." Max implored.

"Why are you making it sound like I was some fan girl? I said the girl could sing. Many people in Nashville can sing." Phaedra scowled.

Max grinned as he put his arm around her and pulled her closer before he tickled her side. "C'mon, Eli. Help me convince her. Willow. Willow. Willow." He began to chant and soon Mathilda and Morgana were chanting right along with him.

When he looked in her direction, she was staring at him. He met her stare. Despite what happened in the meadow he wouldn't back down. The way her eyes held his suggested her wish and hope was for him to ask her to serenade them. He couldn't. Knowing it's what she wanted made him look away.

"Play something for us." Mathilda begged.

Willow looked sad and disappointed. Without saying a word, she got up and disappeared inside the RV. Several seconds later, she appeared with her guitar in her hands. She took her seat and spent some time tuning the guitar. Everyone watched her in silence.

After taking a beat, she played a few chords and then sang 'That Old Black Magic.' Her singing and playing entranced them. She put on a private show just for them. The minute she started to sing, he couldn't take his eyes from her. Under the moonlight, she was ethereal. What no one knew was he'd stood at the back of many smoky, crowded bars and listened to her. He knew he shouldn't, but he'd wanted to hear what he'd be depriving the world. He wished she understood the pain it caused him to keep what she so rightly deserved away from her.

After she finished that song she went right into playing The Police's 'Every Little Thing She Does Is Magic,' but she changed 'she' in the song to 'he.' The more he listened to the lyrics the more uncomfortable he became, and he shifted his seating position several times. When it ended everyone applauded and called out for her to sing more.

"Encore!" Mathilda shouted and cheered. "You're so good."

He clapped along so he wouldn't draw attention to himself, but he wanted to be anywhere, but there at the moment. There was no way he could handle anymore singing tonight. He stood. "Excuse me."

Inside the RV, he made a beeline for the bathroom. After shutting the door he sat on top of the toilet lid. It wasn't long before he realized he made a mistake coming in here. She slept here. He shook his head before he dropped it into his hands. When it came to her, he didn't think clearly. That had to stop. Those kinds of mistakes got people killed. He'd remove himself from the trainings and supervise from afar. Problem solved.

When he exited the bathroom he collided with Willow.

"Sorry."

"Excuse me."

They both spoke at the same time.

A quick step back caused him to bang his head against the door, which swung closed behind him. He winced.

"Are you okay?" She reached for him.

"I'm fine." With nowhere to go, he could only press himself further into the door to avoid her touch.

Her face dropped, and he realized the words came out harsher than they should have. "Sorry, I..."

She put up her hand. "I'm tired. I'm going to bed." Squeezing past him, she walked into the bedroom and slid the door shut without a backward glance.

For a while, he stood in the same spot and looked at the closed door, wishing that whole exchange had gone differently.

Once he left the motor home, he avoided the others and put his sleeping bag further away from the fire. He punched his pillow to fluff it up, but also out of frustration. Grass and leaves rustled a short while later as someone approached.

"I thought everyone would have gotten the hint I wanted to be alone." He still hadn't seen who was coming in his direction, but he had a good guess. When Zoriana sat, it surprised him.

"You're not who I expected." He mumbled, lay back on his pillow and looked at her. "Wanna talk about it?"

Zoriana slid off the log she was sitting on and landed with a plop, onto the dirt-packed ground. She said nothing for several moments, only stared into the distance. "She hates me."

He sat up and took her hands in his.

"She doesn't hate you... she just found out that her mother had a life before her, has a past she may not get to learn about... that's tough for a kid. I think we forget she's only seventeen."

"You're being kind." She chuckled mirthlessly and looked at their joined hands.

"I shouldn't have hit her." Tears clogged her throat.

"No, you shouldn't."

"It's just... you know where that kind of curiosity leads. I had a front-row seat when the rebellion had to be suppressed." A bitter note marked her words.

He stared into the shadows. That dark time in their coven's history was still casting a long shadow.

"I know it's not something that's talked about, but it might help things between the two of you if you explained that to her."

Zoriana nodded. A lengthy silence passed between them. She sniffled. "By the way, who did you think I was?"

"Hmm?" He answered absently, his attention elsewhere.

"When I came over here, you mentioned I wasn't who you were expecting. Who did you think I was?"

Oh that.

"No one. It doesn't matter." If he told her, she'd only ask more questions, and he didn't want to be grilled tonight. For once, Zoriana asked nothing further, too lost in her own troubles.

***

The next morning, the escalating, heated argument taking place between Zoriana and Mathilda on the fringes of the camp awoke him. He dragged himself over to the fire in search of caffeine while he rubbed his eyes. Phaedra and Max were eating breakfast and pretending not to listen. His gaze drifted to the motor home, where he assumed Willow was still sleeping or avoiding him or the ugly quarrel that was happening or both.

"Where's Morgana?" He sipped at the hot coffee. It burned going down his throat, but he welcomed the caffeine that should kick in and wake him up in a few minutes.

"She's out picking herbs and practicing spells." Phaedra said the words, but kept her eyes glued on the mother and daughter who didn't seem to be ending their fight anytime soon.

"Shouldn't we stop them?" Max looked between Eli and Phaedra concerned.

"No." They both answered in unison.

"They need to fight." Eli sipped more coffee and scrounged for breakfast.

"Yeah, let them get out everything between them so we can avoid these awkward conversations where they talk around each other or pass messages. That shit has to stop." Phaedra resumed eating her food.

Eli smirked at Phaedra's no-nonsense approach on how to deal with the issue between Zoriana and Mathilda.

Several minutes passed and the angry words died away, replaced by sniffles. Mathilda walked into the woods.

Distress was etched into Zoriana's face. It was obvious nothing was resolved. He looked elsewhere when she approached to afford her some privacy and give her the illusion they hadn't just be an audience to yet another blow-up between her and her daughter. It was hard on all of them, seeing the two argue when they were so close. It was strange.

Zoriana reached the fire and sat heavily onto a stump. On their way to the stream to clean their dishes, Phaedra squeezed her shoulder. She patted Phaedra's hand in thanks.

Before he could say anything, Willow chose that moment to emerge from the motor home. She looked bright-eyed and ready to take charge of her day. Whatever he was about to say to Zoriana was forgotten.

CHAPTER 13

Willow

IT WAS PAINFUL hearing the irritation and hostility that volleyed back and forth between Mathilda and Zoriana. Whenever she used to come into the coffee shop, they were always so close. Often she looked at their relationship and wished for the millionth time that her own mother were still alive. The pang she experienced at the widening rift between the two was hard to shake, but when it came to families, she believed you had to let them work it out.

Once she heard the angry stomp of Mathilda's Dr. Martens, she pushed those feelings to the back of her mind and put on her game face. She was sorry for what Zoriana and Mathilda were going through, but she had to focus on honing her powers so she stood a chance against Killian.

Eli was alone at the fire when she exited the RV.

Great.

The last thing he seemed to want was for the two of them to be unchaperoned. Yes, Zoriana was present, but she wouldn't be taking part in any conversations, which left her to make awkward conversation with him. She was tired of having her feelings hurt. It was hard not to beat a hasty retreat inside the RV and claim she forgot something.

Don't be a coward.

She put one foot in front of the other and walked towards them. "Good morning." She poured herself some coffee. It was no caramel macchiato, but it sufficed.

"Morning." Eli greeted her, but his eyes were now on Zoriana, who was struggling. The woman offered no greeting; she was hurting and lost in her grief.

"Did you want any breakfast?" He asked her after a couple more minutes of eyeing Zoriana with concern.

She shook her head and continued to nurse her coffee.

"Meet me in the meadow in fifteen." He walked away after issuing the order.

It looked like they would be alone again today. That's fine. She could be all business and have laser focus too. It was important to her to master this 'Oracle' ability. She told herself that putting her feelings aside for Eli would be a breeze.

Twenty minutes later, she met him in the meadow. He did a decent job at seething without showing it, but not great. It was clear; it pissed him off she was purposefully late. His nostrils flared in agitation and he wouldn't look at her.

Dropping to the ground, she sat cross-legged in front of him and tried not to simper. It was hard not to let the satisfaction show.

Eli got right down to business. "Close your eyes." He bit out the words.

She closed her eyes and relaxed her body and centered her thoughts on remembering what she'd done last time to see the flashes of images.

"Deep breaths." His tone grew softer.

She followed his advice. While she maintained the breathing pattern she tried to clear her mind and became frustrated when it didn't happen easily.

"Ugh!" Her eyes flew open, and she slapped the grass. "Why can't this be easier? If I'm the Oracle, why doesn't this just come naturally?" The whining sounded pathetic even to her own ears, but she couldn't help the way she felt. Her eyes skittered everywhere and refused to meet his gaze. She knew he was observing her because her cheeks and the tops of her ears burned.

The silence was unbearable, so she peeked at him. Just like she thought, he was watching her. "What?" It was hard not to twist a little attitude around her words.

Still, he said nothing.

She sighed and stared back at him.

"I know you're anxious for it to happen, but at the beginning it may come in fits and starts... remember for twenty-six years you haven't tapped into your power. It will take time. Be patient with yourself." There was no snarkiness or impatience in his tone. He sounded understanding, and it made her feel like a brat.

Lowering her gaze to the ground, she tugged a few blades of grass from the earth and rolled them between her fingers. "How are you so calm?"

"Years of practice." He smiled. "We don't come out of the womb knowing how to be witches, it takes study and practice."

This comment caused her to smile back at him. Some of the tension left her shoulders.

"Do you want to try again?"

She looked off across the clearing, thinking it over before she returned her gaze to him. "Can I have some time to get my head straight?" Things were going well between them at this moment and she hoped her request for a break wouldn't upset him.

"Yeah, go on. I'm going to stay here and meditate. Come back in thirty." He shut his eyes and let out a slow breath like he'd been teaching her.

For a minute she watched him, but then realized it wouldn't take long before he knew she hadn't left. If he opened his eyes and caught her staring, he might pull away from her even more. She scrambled to stand up and then walked back to camp.

Once she returned she saw Morgana sitting alone near the fire, sorting through a bunch of wild plants.

"Hey."

"Hey." Morgana answered with a grin.

"Where is everyone?" Willow looked around. The place was deserted. She sat on a log nearby.

"Mathilda's inside the RV, Zoriana is off somewhere." She searched around like she was trying to remember which direction she headed. "Phaedra and Max are off someplace, probably making out." She joked, and they both giggled.

"What's all this?" Willow waved her hand toward the plants and flowers surrounding Morgana.

"Herbs and plants for magic spells. It's always good to stock up when I have the opportunity."

Willow nodded.

"Where's Eli?"

"Oh, he preferred to stay in the meadow and meditate. We'll resume my training later. I needed a break."

Morgana continued to work and a brief silence lapsed between them before she spoke again. "You know, I wanted to apologize for my role in lying to you. We were neighbors and hung out... I know it's part of the job, but I'm sorry I lied to you."

The admission surprised Willow and left her speechless. "Um... I appreciate that. Thank you." She wasn't sure what to say. "I think I will rest before I have to meet up with Eli again." The smile on her face seemed false. She appreciated Morgana's apology, but remembering the life she had before all of this happened was still raw some days. The constant reminder was like having salt poured on an open wound.

She was almost to the motor home when two people appeared out of thin air right in front of her. When she whirled around, she realized there were three in total. She wasn't sure who they were, but she had an idea. After getting over the initial shock, she found her voice and yelled for anyone to hear her.

Mathilda busted out of RV seconds after she screamed. Instantly, she hurled a fire bolt from her hand. One intruder jumped out of the way, narrowly missing being engulfed in flames. Morgana was engaged in combat with the other two. Willow did the only thing she could think of and hid beneath the RV. As she cowered underneath the vehicle, she watched the witches fight, who she was sure were vampires, Killian's minions.

She was helpless to defend herself against the supernaturals. Other people fought her battles, and it infuriated her that she was of no help. Then she remembered the weapons and other hardware they acquired from Samson. While Mathilda and Morgana kept the others engaged in combat, she scrambled out from under the RV and ran inside. She hoped to find one of the guns or the supernatural grenade launchers. Frantically, she searched. While she hunted she realized she needed to tell Eli what was happening, so he'd return to camp.

Please let this work.

It surprised him when she could do it last time so she could only pray it worked now.

'WE'RE IN TROUBLE. COME QUICK.' She sent the telepathic message, hoping Eli received it, while she continued her search for one of the weapons.

Got it.

She pulled it free. Thankfully, she pulled the right one she realized, remembering the weapon when Samson displayed it with pride at his warehouse.

You can do this.

Adrenaline coursed through her veins and she hoped the mental pep talk made her feel like Ripley from *Aliens*.

"One... two... three..." She kicked the door open and kept her finger on the trigger firing multiple vervain grenades. Soon, a fine mist of spray clouded the air. They were definitely vampires, because the vervain had an instant effect on them, their skin reacted like they had received an acid burn. Just as they started to stagger around, Phaedra came charging in with a mighty roar, shouting words she couldn't decipher. She twisted and pointed her fingers in the direction of one of the vampires. The minute she did this, it made the vampire's neck snap. They fell to the ground unconscious.

Willow's eyes became as big as saucers when she saw Max run towards the fallen vampire. But he wasn't in human form or dog form. He was a mix of man and wolf, a hybrid of sorts. His body was large in stature with the head of a wolf. The musculature of his arms and torso were that of a man's and covered in fur. He stood on the hind legs of a wolf and had deadly claws. With his superhuman strength he hefted the unconscious vampire into the air and plunged his sharp canines into their throat, then ripped the head from the torso. Once he did so, he threw the decapitated head and carcass away from him like it weighed nothing. Then he tipped his head back and let out a howl that raised the hairs all over her body.

Morgana, Phaedra and Mathilda dispatched another vampire by setting him ablaze. When she looked around, the third one had fled. She dropped to the ground and panted. Her heart was in her throat and the beating was so loud, for a minute it was the only sound she could hear. It was a while before she processed Phaedra standing next to her, calling her name. Morgana and Mathilda showed concern. When she looked up, Max had even returned to human Max and was wrapped in a blanket with blood staining his mouth. She glanced at everyone in a daze. Her eyes landed back on Phaedra.

"I think you went into shock."

"I'm okay." When she stumbled to her feet, she didn't protest when Phaedra reached out a hand to steady her.

"What happened?" Eli's voice rang out in disbelief and concern. He stood over the charred remains of the vampire they had roasted.

"I tried to reach you, but I guess it didn't work." Shame and disgust ate at her and she averted her gaze. "I'm sorry I wasn't any help." She mumbled and wrapped her arms around her body.

"Are you kidding?" Morgana came closer and gripped her by her arms. "If you hadn't thought to run in and find the Vervain Launcher, we may not have gained the upper-hand. It was your quick thinking that turned the tide on their ambush." She squeezed her biceps and offered her a warm, reassuring smile.

Eli walked towards the group wearing a grim expression. "At least this confirms they are working with a witch. How else would they have been able to get around our cloaking spell?" His eyes sought hers. "You okay?"

She nodded. "Just trying to understand why I could talk inside your mind the other day and today... nothing."

"What did I tell you? Don't beat yourself up. That night you weren't afraid. Having to use your abilities under pressure in a life or death situation takes practice... I'll teach you..." He made a move towards her and then caught himself. "I'm glad you're okay." His eyes were still locked on hers as he rubbed the back of his neck. After a few more seconds, he looked away and spoke to the group. "We're leaving tonight. It's not safe here anymore."

"Mathilda?" Everybody turned to find Zoriana rushing towards them. She dropped whatever she'd been carrying. "Is anyone hurt? Is everyone okay?" She meant the questions for all, but her eyes zeroed in on Mathilda and raked her body, checking for injuries. Willow half expected her to perform a physical examination. It seemed the only way she would be satisfied her daughter was unharmed.

Zoriana took more steps towards Mathilda and reached out her open arms to hug her when the girl stepped back.

"I'm fine." Mathilda's voice was a mix of hostility and embarrassment. Anyone could see how badly Zoriana wanted to hold her daughter. Her arms twitched. Maybe she sensed her mother's need too, because she stepped forward and let her mother embrace her. The whole time her arms hung limp at her sides. Once she deemed it enough, she pried herself from her mother's grip and walked away.

"I'm gonna put on some clothes. Man, I'm bummed. I liked those cargo shorts." Max muttered on his way inside the trailer. Leave it to Max to bring some levity to the situation.

Phaedra and Morgana dragged the bodies onto the flames so they burned to ash. Willow assisted them in packing up camp. The shock was taking its time to wear off. She was glad she was working alone so she could freak out on the inside and get herself together. Taking down the tent allowed her to focus on something else. She took a few deep breaths using the technique Eli had taught her and found it helped tremendously.

CHAPTER 14

Eli

AS THEY DROVE, he beat himself up over not being there to protect her. He shouldn't have stayed out in the meadow. When she headed back to camp, he should have gone with her. It was hard not to lose himself amidst the tangle of guilt.

They used magic to load the RV, so they could get on the road faster. For the last two hours, they'd driven aimlessly. Thirty minutes ago, he'd decided where they were headed, but hadn't voiced it aloud. "Head to the coven."

"What? Are you sure?" Phaedra eyed him for confirmation.

"After what just happened, we need to brief the Elders."

Unlike the other times when they traveled, no card games were taking place and no girl talk was exchanged.

Willow wasn't strumming her guitar, and she stayed in the bedroom with the door closed. He wasn't sure if she was sleeping or still trying to process what happened. It was silent.

Phaedra turned the vehicle off onto another road to head toward their coven.

If they hadn't been ambushed, he would have communicated with the Elders the way they always did. Given there may be a mole working with Killian, they had to be careful. A face-to-face was required.

They had over a thousand miles to go to reach Salem. When Phaedra tired at six hundred miles into the journey, Eli took over driving so she could rest. Everyone slept as he drove the dark back road. Night had descended an hour ago. He had no co-pilot, but he enjoyed the solitude and pondering their return to the coven. It had been a while since he'd been home.

"Hey" Willow whispered when she sat in the passenger seat.

He gave her a quick look, before he returned his attention to the road. "I thought everyone was asleep."

"I was... I just woke up and saw there was no one keeping you company." She yawned and stretched her limbs like a graceful cat. "Where are we heading?"

"To the coven."

"Is it because of what happened?"

He was silent for a beat. "Yeah... it's not safe to communicate in the usual way right now."

She stared out the windshield with a vacant look on her face.

"What are you thinking about?"

"That you still haven't shown me any magic." She smiled an impish grin.

He chuckled. "What are you talking about? I disappeared and reappeared behind you the day we started your combat training."

"That doesn't count. Today, I saw Phaedra snap someone's neck using her magic and Mathilda shot a fireball from her hand. You gotta do better than disappearing." She snorted and then giggled as she tucked one leg beneath her.

"Aren't you hard to please?" He teased her.

"You have to wow me." She stuck her tongue out at him playfully and relaxed into the seat.

The quiet enveloped them. It was nice. For once he didn't shy away from being alone with her. After a few minutes, she turned on the radio. She adjusted the volume level so it wouldn't disturb the others. The Cure's 'Lovesong' began to play. The lyrics washed over him and halfway through the song he realized how true they felt.

No.

He couldn't go down that road. It only led to trouble. Without asking he leaned over and turned the station. Glam metal poured from the speakers. He adjusted the volume.

"Hey... don't tell me you're not a fan of The Cure."

"They're cool... it's just ballads make me sleepy. Since I'm driving that might not be the best thing... Plus, the driver always gets dibs on song selection." He smirked.

"I thought it was the person riding shotgun that got control of the playlist?"

"Wrong."

The one-word response cracked her up, and she doubled over in laughter. Her giggle was infectious and seconds later he was laughing too. She recovered after a few minutes.

"How about we take turns picking the music? You pick a song, then I pick one, that way we both get what we want."

He considered her request. "Deal."

When her turn came again, she turned the dial until India.Arie's 'I Am Light,' wafted through the speakers. At first she just hummed, but it wasn't long before the songstress appeared and she was singing along. Her sound was soulful and rich. The notes and melodies she sang wound themselves around his heart. He could listen to it always. Again he was sorry the world would never know her voice.

"I'm sorry." He spoke so low he was unsure she'd heard him until she stopped singing. She didn't ask him why.

"I know." Her response humbled him. Within a few seconds, she resumed.

They went back and forth each taking turns choosing a song. It took another hour before they struck up a conversation and talked off and on during the music for the next few hours. For a while their talk was random, but then she asked about the talisman he wore. "What does your ring symbolize? Does it do something? I've noticed the others wear pieces of jewelry that have the same stone and inscriptions, except Max. I gather it has to do with being a witch?" She leaned her body over the armrest, eager for answers to her questions.

He looked at the ring on the pinky of his right hand. It was made of solid gold with mystical runic symbols carved into it. In the middle was a greenish-colored gemstone. Phaedra wore hers as a medallion hidden underneath her shirt. Mathilda wore hers this way too. Morgana and Zoriana both had theirs fashioned into rings like him. He kept his eyes on the road as he answered her. "It's a talisman. Typically, it's not worn, but since we're always moving about, it helps to wear it as jewelry to keep it near us."

"Okay, but what does it do?"

"It strengthens the magic we do."

"You pull your magic from it?"

"No." He smirked at her inquisitiveness. "This isn't a source we can pull magic from per se, it just strengthens it, enhances it. Sometimes we draw from the elements, the earth or our ancestors. It depends on what we're trying to do." He faced her. "But magic comes at a cost." He looked back at the road. "Since we're hereditary witches, there's a lot of magic that..." Willow cut him off.

"Wait. Hold the phone." She put her hand up in a gesture meant to silence him. "What does that mean? Hereditary witch."

He hadn't realized when he woke up this morning he'd end up giving her a lesson on witchcraft. "The Walker bloodline is centuries old, because of that, most of us were born with magic. Learning how to use it came easier than someone that's a student." When he looked over at her, he saw her expression telling him he had to elaborate. "Students are witches that only have magic by training and studying." Another glance at her revealed, the gears in her mind turning. He was certain she was planning her next question.

"Zoriana and Phaedra aren't Walkers by blood. Are they hereditary witches?"

If she leaned on the decades old armrest anymore he's afraid she would fall onto the floor, but he kept his mouth shut and answered. "Yes. Phaedra is a descendant of

Tituba, a slave woman who confessed to being a witch during the Salem witch trials and gained her freedom. Zoriana is descended from a family of witches that survived and fled Spain during the Basque witch trials that happened during the Spanish Inquisition. Morgana is not a Walker by birth either, but she's a hereditary witch. I'm not sure of her lineage. I just know the coven adopted her when her mother died." He let the silence settle between them for a moment before he spoke again. "None of us could be Protectors without having hereditary magic."

"Because you're more powerful?"

He nodded. She seemed satisfied with their Q & A session and resumed listening to the music.

An hour later, his song ended, and it was her turn to select the next one. When she hadn't done so, he glanced over and found her asleep. In sleep, she looked peaceful. He turned the volume lower and concentrated on the road. His thoughts returned to home, the thing he'd been thinking about before she showed up to keep him company. He wasn't certain what kind of reception their homecoming would receive.

They hadn't sent word they were coming, but he was sure they knew. Maybe they had an idea who was helping Killian. Whether or not they had something, he needed to come up with a plan. They couldn't hide out at the coven forever. It put too many people in danger.

CHAPTER 15

Willow

BY THE TIME they hit the outskirts of Salem, Zoriana was behind the wheel and Morgana rode shotgun. Everyone stared out the windows and watched fields turn into buildings and neighborhoods the closer they got to home.

"Wasn't sure when we'd see this place again." It was unclear by her tone whether she was glad to be home.

Willow squeezed in next to Phaedra, her head swiveled this way and that as she peered at the city. "I've never been to Massachusetts."

Minutes later, they pulled up to a large, three-story, dark grey, clapboard mansion that featured First Period architecture. Plumes of smoke curled out of the central chimney, even though it was a warm spring day. They piled out of the motor home and stood ogling the house for several seconds.

Like other homes in the neighborhood, it was nondescript. Despite that, Willow found herself drawn to the house.

"Wow." Awe colored her voice. She gazed at the home in adoration before glancing up and down the street. "These houses are so interesting. You don't see this kind of architecture everywhere."

"If you're impressed by this, wait until you get a look inside the place." Mathilda winked at her.

Everyone snickered.

"What? What about the inside?"

Eli smirked. "You'll see."

"Huh?"

"Nevermind."

He led them up the steps to a monstrous oaken door with a large, round, iron knocker and removed a wooden key from his pocket that resembled the wood of the door. A keyhole appeared, and he inserted it into the lock. It twisted itself and the door swung open. Everyone stepped inside to a darkened lobby. A long corridor stretched out ahead of them with doors lining the hallway. Willow peered over his shoulder and tried to look around despite the lack of adequate light. Eli didn't make a move to walk further into the house or enter one of the many doors.

"Why are we just standing here?" She whispered.

"We're waiting for someone to come and collect us." Amusement colored his words. "And why are you whispering?"

She shrugged. "It's so quiet. It felt like the right thing to do."

Footsteps shuffled along the corridor towards them. Talking ceased as they waited for the person to approach.

"They sent me to bring you to the Elders." The wizened old man had shocking white hair that stuck out this way and that like he was constantly pulling on it and he wore spectacles and a robe that swept the floor.

"Hello to you too, Archie." Eli greeted the curmudgeon and chuckled.

The man harrumphed and walked back the way he'd come expecting them to follow.

"You know he hates that." Zoriana hissed.

"Why?" Willow whispered again, not wanting Archie to overhear her.

"He prefers his full name, Archibald. Eli's been calling him Archie since he was a kid because he knows the old man despises it." Zoriana explained.

They walked for forever and then Archibald opened a door that stood at the end of the corridor and a blinding light lit up the doorway. Everyone trudged through, but Willow hung back, hesitant.

"There's no reason to be afraid." Eli tried to soothe her. He grinned and walked through. She took a deep breath and followed.

Once they entered, she got a glimpse of the robe the old man wore that she couldn't see in the darkened hallway. It changed color when he moved and depending on the way the light hit it. It had zodiac signs and other symbols decorating the surface.

When she stopped eyeing the garment and looked around her mouth dropped open in shock and she halted in her tracks. They were standing in what resembled a town square, complete with a gazebo in the center. Lush greenery and benches decorated the space. Numerous floating doors that entered to nothing encircled the perimeter.

How can this be inside the house?

People milled about. The dress was a mixture of various robes much like Archibald's and everyday clothing.

"How is this possible?" Her eyes couldn't stop darting this way and that.

"The house acts as a portal to our community." Eli stopped next to her and smiled. It was a look that encompassed nostalgia and the recollection of fond memories. "Depending on how long we're here, maybe you'll get a tour and a history lesson."

"Really?" She couldn't quell the hopefulness in her voice. The thought of exploring the place made her feel like a kid.

"We'll see." He fought the grin that tugged at the corner of his lip.

"C'mon, they aren't gonna wait all day." Archibald called out.

In her excitement over seeing her new surroundings she'd forgotten their visit had a purpose.

There was a noticeable shift in Eli's demeanor when the Elders were mentioned. She didn't have time to ask about it as they jogged to catch up with the group. Archibald led them to a door that was taller than the others. This must be where the Elders convened. He opened it and ushered them in. She was the last one into the chamber. Inside, the windowless space was lit only by candlelight. A raised dais with a long sturdy wooden table and chairs took up a whole wall. No other furniture decorated the room.

Seated on the platform were thirteen men and women clad in robes. The middle seat was larger and more ornate than the other twelve. A tall, dark-haired man with gray in the temples stood in front of that chair. It was clear he was the authority in the room. He looked at her.

"My name is Silas and I am the Interim Chief Elder. Cora who is the oldest among us, is the current Chief Elder, but illness has her bed-ridden."

There's someone older than Archibald?

The woman was sick and here she was making jokes. She still couldn't help wondering about the woman's age.

"I'm guessing you already know my name." She was suspicious of the Council. While she'd gotten to know the motley crew of witches and the werewolf that were tasked with her protection, the Elders were virtual strangers to her. For all she knew, a member of the Council was responsible for Killian locating them. She felt justified in being distrustful.

"We do, Willow." His piercing eyes never left her face.

Eli stepped forward. "Sorry we couldn't send word of our arrival, but they attacked us. I'm afraid it's what we've feared... a witch is working with Killian. There's no other way they could have known our location. I didn't want to send a message in case someone intercepted it."

There was some mumbling among the other Elders at his statement. Silas eyes lingered on her for a moment before he redirected his attention onto Eli. He stood taller under Silas' penetrating gaze. The rest of the group was silent behind him.

"Yes, an update or word of warning is the protocol..."

Willow noticed Eli's body go rigid and his fists clenched at his sides in response.

"I guess... given the circumstances, we understand." A tense silence followed before Silas spoke again. "We have much to discuss and you have traveled a long way, why don't you refresh yourselves and tomorrow we'll talk."

Archibald herded them from the room and back into the square, then left. Eli and Phaedra moved away from the group talking in hushed whispers.

"He seems like a barrel of laughs." Willow murmured to Mathilda in a sarcastic tone.

"Silas is Eli's father."

Willow's eyes darted over to Eli, who was still in a heated discussion with Phaedra. "Oh."

"He's my uncle. My dad is his brother."

Willow blanched, and Mathilda giggled. "It's okay. I don't take offense. I know how tough he can be."

What was life like growing up with a father like that? She wondered as she looked back at Eli.

Five minutes later, Eli and Phaedra approached the group and showed no signs of whatever quarrel they had moments ago.

"Eat, find rooms and rest. We're not here for a vacation. Tomorrow we resume training: combat, spells... Willow, you and I will work on your Oracle abilities."

He sounded like he was getting them ready for a big high school football game. The pep talk ended and everyone split off: Phaedra and Max walked away together, and Morgana, Zoriana and Mathilda each went in a different direction. Willow didn't know what to do. When she looked up and found Eli still standing close by she sighed in relief. "How do I find a room?"

"Come on. I'll show you."

She followed beside him, casting furtive glances his way. "So, that's your father."

"Yep." He didn't look at her. He just kept walking.

It didn't seem like he wanted to talk about it so she dropped that line of conversation and tried to go for funny. "If Archibald isn't the oldest person here, and he looks like that, what does Cora look like?" She bit her lip and waited for a response.

A grin broke out across his face and he looked at her. "Old."

They both laughed. The knot in her stomach eased. It was nice when it was easy between them. She hoped being at the coven wouldn't further complicate things.

Eli took them back through the door Archibald led them through earlier. In the long corridor, she wondered how anyone knew which door led where since they all looked alike.

They walked five doors down. On the right side of the hall he turned a knob. She stepped through after him and found herself in a sitting area decorated in deep blues. The suite contained an 18th century velvet upholstered Chippendale sofa and Queen Anne style furnishings that boasted claw footed legs. In the regal room she felt like royalty.

She followed behind him where he opened a door to a bedroom swathed in beige and white. A huge canopied bed with curtains was the centerpiece. More Queen Anne style furnishings decorated the space.

"The rooms are old-fashioned, but I assure you the mattress is not from the 18th century." He joked.

She giggled. "Good to know." She hopped on the bed to test it. "Very comfy."

Eli cleared his throat. "You can rest if you like or I can show you how to locate the kitchens."

She yawned and scooted back towards the pillows. "Sleep now, food later." After stretching, she folded her hands beneath her head on the pillow. She hadn't realized how exhausted she was until her body touched the bed. As she drifted off, she heard Eli's voice. "Sweet dreams."

CHAPTER 16

Eli

AFTER HE LEFT a sleeping Willow, he went in search of his father. This homecoming was already off to a great start. He'd called him out on protocol in front of the whole Council of Elders. He tolerated his father's disdain in private, but he wouldn't tolerate it in public.

In the field, he had to make the calls that kept everyone safe and sometimes that meant procedure couldn't always be followed. His father knew that. "Why do you insist on treating me like I haven't earned the right to be treated as the head of the Protectors?" He stormed into his parents' suite and slammed the door.

"Hello, dear." His mother, Josephine greeted him. "It's nice to have you home for a while."

Silas was removing his robe and hanging it on a hook. "Well, if you insist on acting like a petulant child, maybe I'm correct in how I've handled things."

With his hands stuffed deep in his pockets, he paced the floor and glowered at his father. Phaedra tried to convince him to hold off on the confrontation, but he was too stubborn to listen to her. He wondered if she was right.

"Argue later you two... come sit and have dinner. When was the last time you ate?" In the kitchen, Josephine had a pot boiling something on the stove and the oven door opened on its own so a floating casserole dish could slide onto the wire rack. A knife chopped various vegetables on a cutting board. This happened in the kitchen while his mother was seated at the dining room table typing on her laptop. Her glasses perched on the edge of her nose as she stared at the screen.

The sullen demeanor lingered as he pulled out a chair and sat. He hated that every time he was around his father he reverted to adolescence. Back then he was anxious for his father's approval and acceptance. Now he just wanted him to respect that he was more than capable of handling the duties of leading the Protectors. He opened his mouth to say something.

"Uh-uh. After dinner. No Council or Protector talk until then." Her eyes never left the computer screen.

Ten minutes later, they were eating the meal prepared using magic.

"I've heard the Oracle is quite the looker."

Out of the corner of his eye, Eli caught his father's sharp look of disapproval. "Mom, it's forbidden for..."

She interrupted him. "I think it's a stupid rule. That commandment should never have been approved in the first place, but what do I know."

Eli was grateful his mother stopped talking after that. The rest of the meal passed in silence. He waited until he and his father were in the office to resume the conversation he started when he first arrived.

"Why do we go through this every time?" He leaned on the desk as he addressed him.

Silas stood behind it and gave him a condescending staredown. "I will not give you special treatment, because I'm your father."

"Damn it!" He pounded his fist on the oak surface that sat between them. "I'm not asking for special treatment, just to be treated with respect." Fury and indignation seeped from his pores as he glowered at his father.

"State the Protector's Commandments." The order came out of nowhere.

"What?" Some of his rage dissipated while he wondered about the purpose of his father's demand. "I know the Commandments." His tone wasn't as sure as it was moments ago and it had nothing to do with whether he knew them, but why his father asked.

"Go on then." His father pinned him with a hard stare and waited.

He recited the Protector's Commandments. "A Protector shall defend and protect the Oracle at all costs. A Protector shall always have his comrade's back." His nostrils flared in agitation and he continued rattling off the commandments. "A Protector, if they be a witch must have hereditary magic. A Protector shall never disclose their true identity to the Oracle. A Protector shall never reveal her lineage to an unknowing Oracle." He paused.

"The final commandment."

He gave his father a death stare, and he clenched his fists. "A Protector shall not enter a relationship or fall in love with the Oracle."

"Why was the last commandment approved?"

Through gritted teeth he huffed out the answer. "Because the Congress of Supernatural Beings agreed no one with supernatural abilities should enter a relationship or procreate with the Oracle. Doing so might cause her to offer her powers in allegiance to the group of her suitor." He said the words as if he was reading them straight from a textbook or constitution.

"How many of the commandments have you broken?" The contempt in his father's voice was devoid of subtlety.

Eli said nothing. His father had walked him into a trap from which there was no escape.

"You walk into my house full of anger over me questioning you when your actions give me every reason to remove you from the Protectors."

Eli sighed. "I explained why we had to go against protocol. I'm not purposefully trying to disobey orders or the commandments." He hated that he had this childish need to justify himself to his father.

Why do I even bother?

Agonizing seconds ticked by as he stared into his father's eyes and wondered why he kept going back and forth with him. They'd continued this struggle for years and nothing had ever changed. The fight left him. He was done. Without a word, he walked out of the room.

***

He'd find Phaedra and see if she wanted to drink with him. When he knocked on her door, she took awhile to answer. He almost gave up. The door opened a crack and she growled at him, "What do you want?"

He pushed past her into the room, oblivious. "I found some of that apple brandy you like so much in Archie's stash. The one where Lavinia grows the apple in the bottle so it makes the best stuff. Thought we could get shit-faced together." When he turned to face her, he saw she only wore a kimono, which she now belted to cover her nakedness.

"Oh." He deflated.

Max called out. "Did you get rid of him?"

She gave Eli a displeased look and walked to the bedroom. "Give us a minute, okay." She closed the door on Max without waiting for an answer.

"I advised you not to do it. This happens every time." Her voice was not sympathetic.

He dropped onto her sofa and rolled the bottle between his hands. "I can always count on you to say, 'I told you so.'" The sarcasm dripped from his words. What did he expect? It was Phaedra. She didn't coddle. He needed his friend to talk some sense into him... again.

"Everyone knows your father is a hard man... you don't need his approval. It's easier to hear than to accept. I get it, but dude..."

"Dude?" He laughed. "I think you've been hanging around Max too much."

Phaedra snorted. "Don't deflect. I was going to say you're a grown ass man. Get over it." She patted his knee and stood. "Now it's time for you to go."

He chuckled. "You're kicking me out? I understand." He stood. "Can you make sure everyone knows we're getting started early tomorrow?"

"I got you covered."

"Here." He placed the bottle of apple brandy on the coffee table. "You keep it. I know how much you like it."

"I would have taken it from you, anyway." They both laughed as she led him to the door.

"Oh and try not to wear out Max. No complaints about being too sore or cramped from you either." The joke earned him a playful punch to his bicep, but coming from Phaedra there was nothing wimpy about it and he rubbed his arm. She punched him a second time.

"Ow. What was that one for?"

"That was for interrupting us." The door slammed in his face.

He continued rubbing his arm as he walked away. When he rounded the corner he collided with Archibald. "Cora wants you to bring the Oracle to see her." He stated the order and kept moving.

Eli watched him leave and shook his head, wondering what Cora wanted with Willow.

CHAPTER 17

Willow

"WILLOW. WILLOW."

Someone was calling her name she realized when she opened her eyes. She turned to find Eli next to her bed. "I need you to come with me."

She blinked, trying to wake herself and clear the cobwebs from her brain. "Come with you where?" She peered at him and rubbed her throat. Her mouth was dry. As the drowsy fog lifted, she realized she was talking to Eli and might have morning breath since she'd just woken from a nap. Her hand flew up in front of her mouth. The bag that had her toothbrush and other toiletries was still on the RV. "Where are we going? I should freshen up, but I don't have my bag." She spoke from behind her hand.

He chuckled. "Don't worry, you can put your hand down. Your breath doesn't smell." He left the bedroom and came back a few seconds later with her bag over his shoulder. "I grabbed it before I got here."

"Thank..." She put her hand down, feeling dumb after him laughing at her. "You."

"Hurry and shower, change or whatever you need to do, because we have to get moving. I'll wait for you right out here." Without waiting for her to respond, he walked into the adjacent sitting room.

Who're we in a rush to see?

She got off the bed and took her bag into the adjoining bathroom she hadn't checked out yet. There was a large claw-footed tub that at some point she hoped she could make use of. The separate shower was one of the few modern amenities in the suite. Perusal of the bathroom would have to wait, since Eli was in a hurry. She made short work of getting ready.

When she walked into the sitting room, he rose to his feet. "You look nice."

She wore black, slim fitting, ankle length cropped pants and black pointed toe flats. The sleeveless blouse was black and white with a Peter Pan collar.

"Thank you... I wasn't sure who we were meeting, so..." She trailed off, waiting for him to fill her in on the details. When he still offered no clues she continued.

"Plus, you always look so put together, I didn't want to look like a peasant compared to you." She gestured at his usual attire of dress pants and a collared shirt. This made him laugh as he held the door open for her. She smiled and stepped into the hallway.

"Peasant." He said with amusement still coloring his voice when he stepped out behind her and shut the door.

"Do I need a key or fob or anything?" She glanced at the unlocked door concerned.

"No, it's fine."

"My stuff is in there. Is it safe?" She looked back at him and saw him smirk.

"It'll be fine." He walked down the hallway towards the door at the end, which led to the square.

She hurried along behind him. "You still haven't told me who we're going to see."

He slowed his step, so they were walking beside each other. "Cora, the Chief Elder requested a meeting with you. I'm taking you to her bedchamber."

"Glad I dressed to impress." She smoothed the front of her shirt and touched her hair, wondering if she should have spent more time on it.

"You look great." He reassured her.

"Thanks." It was hard to keep his compliment from making her blush. "It's not every day you meet the Chief Elder of a Coven of Witches." She chuckled and avoided looking at him.

They hadn't fought, and he hadn't rejected her since the drive here. She didn't want to question why he was being so nice. She'd just enjoy it. Hopefully, it would stay this way.

In a corner of the square, there was a door that looked much like the other ones. He opened it. They stepped into a marbled hall with a few columns. A winding staircase led up to a landing. Neither of them spoke as they ascended the steps. Butterflies fluttered around in her stomach. Her nerves were getting the better of her. Cora was just a woman.

At the top of the stairwell, a small area held a wooden bench. There was one large ornate door. Eli pushed it open and ushered her inside. The chamber was dimly lit.

"I'll be out here."

She turned startled. "You're not coming in with me?"

"She didn't want to see me. Just you... don't worry, she doesn't bite." He whispered the last part and shut the door.

Her feet wouldn't move further into the room until her eyes adjusted. A giant four-poster bed was one of the few pieces of furniture. She squinted towards it.

"Come closer child. Let me get a good look at you." The ancient, weathered voice croaked from the bed.

The unexpected sound nearly caused Willow to jump out of her skin. If Cora was as old as she suspected, how was she going to see her in this lighting? As she edged closer, a warm glow bathed the room. Where it was coming from she didn't know, since she hadn't noticed an overhead light or any lamps.

Once she was at the foot of the bed, she could see Cora propped against the pillows. Lines and wrinkles aged her pale face. Her wispy, snow-white hair hung past her shoulders. She wore a white nightgown that had long sleeves with ruffles on the ends and buttoned at the neck.

Cora patted the side of the bed and Willow felt compelled to honor her request. Everything she'd been taught about not staring went right out the window. She found the old woman so fascinating. Neither of them spoke for long minutes. They just regarded each other.

"You're the spitting image of your mother."

The statement made tears spring up in her eyes.

"You met my mother?" Her voice quivered.

"I did child. When she came to the coven we chatted at great length."

Willow drew closer. Hoping the woman would drop some crumbs of information regarding her mother. Even though it had been seventeen years since her death, she missed her every day.

"Tell me about her." She whispered.

The elderly woman patted her hand. "Let me start from the beginning, with your history... so you can understand who you are."

Cora looked at her so direct, like she was peering into her soul. It made her want to turn away, but she held the woman's gaze once she began to speak.

"Your are a descendant of the Pythia which dates back to 8th century BC. The Pythia were the high priestesses of The Temple of Apollo in ancient Greece. If you've studied history, you might know them as the Oracle of Delphi. The women in your family have all been Oracles."

When Cora paused for a breath, Willow couldn't help, but be skeptical. Plus she was impatient to hear about her mother, not a history lesson.

"So you're telling me I'm descended from some ancient Greek whatever?" She stared at the woman wondering if she could see. "You do realize I'm black?"

The old woman cackled in a way that Willow didn't think she was capable of.

"I may be old, but my eyes are not failing. I'm very aware of what color your skin is." Once the levity passed she continued. "There were regular trade routes between Greece and ancient Egypt that date back to the Bronze Age, my dear. It is not a stretch of the imagination to believe that many Grecians that came for trade might have stayed, found wives and procreated. You are a descendant." She said the last sentence in a tone that brooked no argument.

She coughed. "Could you please get me some water?" Her bony fingers rubbed her throat.

Willow found a pitcher sitting on a side table nearby the bed. She was eager for the woman to continue and hurried to fill the glass. After Cora quenched her thirst she continued. "When your ancestors became slaves and were shipped to America, the gift was forgotten and was no longer discussed from generation to generation. It was lost to you. However, there were those that did not forget the great power of the Oracle. They searched for her. It was years after the Civil War ended that the search turned fruitful when a freed slave, a fortune-teller in Louisiana, turned out to be a true seer. Once the Council investigated, they realized they'd found the Oracle and they must protect her. If the knowledge got out that the Oracle hadn't vanished, but was merely dormant, some would seek to control her power. Thus the Protectors were born." Cora adjusted her position against the pillows.

"Are you okay? Are you comfortable?" Whatever she needed Willow would take care of it. This couldn't end, not yet. She was intrigued and curious. Learning about her history and where she came from felt like it was filling spaces and gaps within her she didn't even know existed.

"I'm fine, dear. Where was I... oh yes... The Walker Coven created The Protectors in the late 1800s. A few select witches trained, bound with the duty to protect the Oracle at all costs. They started rumors to discredit the Oracle. It was important to draw attention away from the truth of her visions. Because of this, somewhere down the line in your ancestry, they stopped believing in the gift. It was always there, but the women remained unaware... until your mother."

When Cora ceased talking at that point Willow wanted to shake her. "What about my mother?" Frustration gripped her in its clutches. "Please, tell me about my mother?"

"Come again another day, child. I'm tired now. An old woman needs her rest." There was no urgency in her to finish her thought or continue with her story. Her eyes closed before she rested her head against the pillow indicating she was done for the time being. The cliffhanger would remain until she felt she was ready to tell it, which could be at least twenty-four agonizing hours.

Reluctant to leave, although she knew she wouldn't get anymore today, Willow walked to the door. Repeatedly she looked back over her shoulder, hoping Cora would suddenly experience a second wind or a dose of energy and be ready to keep going.

When she stepped out of the room and closed the door, Eli was waiting, right where he said he would be. "Are you okay?" He rose and came towards her.

Her mind was swirling with her past and thoughts about what Cora would tell her about her mother. "I'm okay." They walked down the steps.

"Are you hungry? You haven't eaten anything in hours."

She was positive she should be famished, but her stomach was in knots. There was no way she could eat. "I just want to go back to my room, if that's okay."

"Sure."

The trip to her room was silent. Waves of curiosity were coming off Eli like someone with bad body odor, but he kept quiet and didn't ask about their conversation. She was grateful. Right now she wasn't ready to share.

"I'll have Mathilda pick you up for training tomorrow." He told her when he dropped her off.

"Thanks." She was still too distracted to focus.

"Good night."

"Night."

CHAPTER 18

Eli

WHAT DID CORA *say to her?*

He couldn't help, but wonder what had Willow so lost in her thoughts when he left her at her room last night. Usually she was so talkative, so it was odd to have her at such a loss for words.

Sparring with Phaedra and Max early this morning worked up a sweat. Even though they were witches and had magic he believed that they should have combat skills, should the need ever arise when they could not use magic. He mopped his brow with a towel and flipped through a spell book waiting for Mathilda to arrive with Willow.

"Yeah, I spent yesterday with Morgana, mixing potions and learning new spells." Mathilda was excited when she entered. It made him happy to see her smile, but when she didn't mention her mother, it concerned him. Now that they were back at the coven, he needed to speak with his uncle and have him get involved.

"I hope you got something to eat this morning, Willow, because we have a long day ahead of us." He stood from his stooped position and discarded the towel.

Her eyes started at his sneaker covered feet and traveled up his sweatpants to his wife beater. He couldn't read her expression.

"So you do own a pair of sweatpants. I was beginning to wonder if you were born in dress pants." She smirked.

He shook his head. "I hope you learn as quickly as your smart mouth comes up with witty things to say because we have a lot to cover." The smirk he sported widened, when she lost a little of her bravado. "We'll start with advanced combat training today. First staves and then knives, you need to master how to properly use that dagger." While he spoke he picked up a staff and twirled it expertly with two hands.

Phaedra and Max entered the room wearing workout gear as he demonstrated some moves with the staff.

"Perfect. You're just the person I wanted to help me." He tossed a staff to Max who caught it with one hand.

"This is known as Bojutsu. Watch and then you'll practice before you choose either Mathilda or Phaedra for a sparring partner."

Max stood in front of him. They bowed to one another and then both sprung into action. The wooden sticks flew through the air at blinding speed as they swung them at each another. The 'thwack' of wood smacking against wood reverberated around the room. Max was a great opponent. He moved with grace, effortlessly defending himself against Eli's attack. After five minutes of sparring, they ended in a draw.

His hair was now slick with sweat. He pushed it back out of his face and approached Willow. "Okay, let's go through the moves so you can understand how to hold it and swing it."

For the next hour and a half they trained her in the basic movements. It impressed him that she picked up the maneuvers quicker than he thought she would. It was also obvious that she often let her frustration get the better of her. He knew this from trying to teach her to meditate. It could end up being her weakness if she wasn't careful. "Who do you want for your sparring partner?"

Her eyes darted between Phaedra and Mathilda. "Mathilda."

It was impossible to keep the smirk from his face. She thought she was choosing the easier opponent, but she was in for a surprise. They each pulled a staff from the rack and squared off against each other. The grin Willow sported when they first began was wiped away as Mathilda came at her hard and unrelenting. Most of the training she'd just learned went out the window as she tried to defend herself against Mathilda's vicious assault.

Just as she ended up flat on her back with Mathilda pointing her staff in her face, Zoriana and Morgana arrived.

"Nice of you to join us." He didn't keep the irritation from his voice. They were late.

"You didn't warn her that Mathilda is as good as Max?" Morgana tried to deflect his comment.

Willow turned accusing eyes on him.

"No, I didn't because I wanted to teach her a lesson in underestimating your adversary." He addressed Morgana before turning to Willow and helping her up from the mat. "You chose Mathilda because you thought she was the weaker of the two, but remember, size and strength don't always win a fight. Speed, agility, dexterity and heart are things to keep in mind."

"Sometimes being underestimated can work in your favor." Mathilda grinned at her like the Cheshire cat.

"Let's go again. Ease up a little." He warned Mathilda.

While they sparred, he pulled Zoriana and Morgana to the side. "What happened? Why weren't you guys on time?" He crossed his arms over his chest and awaited their explanation.

Zoriana looked over his shoulder at the sparring match. Without her having to say anything, he knew her focus was on Mathilda.

"It's my fault." Zoriana began. "Ever since our fight, I noticed that Mathilda was at least talking more to Morgana and I was hoping she could help me figure out how to make things better." She looked lost and helpless as she spoke, her eyes constantly returning to her daughter.

Eli was about to ask her what his uncle had to say regarding the matter when she continued. Tears formed in the corners of her eyes. "Alistair said she's a teenager. She's just going through a phase but..." Her dewy eyes looked up into his. "She's never held a grudge this long." Morgana rubbed her back.

"It's okay. Why don't you take a day?"

She allowed Morgana to lead her to the door. It was unlike Mathilda to be this unforgiving with Zoriana. They had one of the closest mother/daughter relationships he'd ever seen. Usually within twenty-four hours they made up. It was killing her. He had to talk some sense into his cousin. She'd punished her enough.

After she left, Phaedra and Morgana trained together while he and Max monitored Willow's training.

Wisps of hair were matted to Willow's reddened face. It was their eleventh match. She was sweating and panting as she wildly swung her staff and charged at Mathilda, only to get knocked down, for what must have been the hundredth time if her punching the mat in anger before returning to her feet was any indication.

"Don't expect to be amazing right away. It's a learning process." He called out to her.

She flipped him the bird and got in a ready stance to fight with Mathilda again. Most people would have been offended, but if he was honest with himself he found her temper a turn on. When she was fiery, he wanted to kiss the anger right out of her. The thought snuffed out like someone blows out a candle flame. Those thoughts and feelings had to be squashed or he would find himself in a world of trouble. He took a moment to collect himself before focusing on the sparring match.

You didn't need to be clairvoyant to know Willow would get taken down again because she was fighting in anger. He let the inevitable happen before he stepped on the mat next to her where she lay supine.

"We've talked about this." He referred to a conversation he had with her during her first session against Phaedra and reached out his hand to help her up, but she pushed it away and got up on her own.

"Okay. Let's take a break. Work on hand-to-hand combat with Max." He motioned Max over. Plus, now was a good time to talk to Mathilda.

You coward. You're trying to escape her.

His inner voice may be right, but space from her was

what he needed. Once Max began instructing Willow he pulled Mathilda across the room.

"I know what you're going to say." Mathilda looked away from him and put her hand on her hip.

"Then why haven't you?"

She shrugged.

"She's hurting you know." He tried to get her to look at him, but she evaded him. "She apologized so why can't it just be done." He'd barely finished when she exploded.

"She humiliated me." The hurt, angry expression that sprang up in her eyes felt all too familiar. "I would think of all people you would understand how that feels."

His cousin was right. He understood her pain. How many times had he endured his father's criticism in front of others and seethed with rage? Zoriana's actions that day had belittled her. She was a Protector and her mother had reprimanded her like a child, even though she would turn eighteen before the year was over. Still, it was uncharacteristic of Mathilda not to extend forgiveness. He wasn't sure how to reach her.

"Could you just..." Whatever else he was about to say was forgotten when a flash of white light erupted out of his periphery and Max flew back against the wall with great force. Both he and Mathilda turned to see Max sliding down the wall and Willow's extended fist glowing a bright white.

What the hell?

CHAPTER 19

Willow

HER HEARTBEAT HAMMERED in her ears. She couldn't stop looking at her hands. They appeared normal. They trembled, but they no longer glowed with an iridescent white light like they had a few seconds ago.

Max lay in a heap against the wall. The others surrounded him. "I'm sorry." She mumbled and kept looking from his crumpled, unconscious body to her hands. "I'm so sorry." Her whole body trembled. "How was I able to do that?"

Eli left the semi-circle they'd formed around Max and approached her cautiously. "How did you do that?"

"I didn't mean to hurt him." Her eyes pleaded with him for understanding. The quiver in her voice grew. "Is he going to be all right?" She was going into full on panic mode as her breath stuttered in her chest and her words came out choppy. "I... I... don't..."

His arms wrapped around her and he pulled her into his chest. "It's okay."

"No!" She pushed and shoved against him, trying to free herself. Any other time, she would have welcomed his touch, craved it in fact, but Max was hurt and it was her fault. It wasn't going to be all right. After a few more seconds of her struggling against him, he released her, and she ran from the room wanting to be anywhere else. She was suffocating on her fear. It was threatening to choke her, unless she got away.

Out in the hall she tried to get her breathing under control.

'WILLOW?' Eli pushed into her mind.

She shook her head and tried to extricate him from her thoughts. Her eyes returned to her hands. No one ever told her she'd be capable of something like that. She flipped them over repeatedly expecting a revelation. Nothing.

She wanted to return and see if Max was okay, but terror filled her. What if they were angry? What if they were scared of her? What if she killed Max?

'WILLOW.' His voice came through again.

It was too much. She needed to get out of here before Eli came to look for her. Right now she didn't want to talk to him. She wanted answers and knew where she would get them.

Retracing their steps from yesterday, she found the door that led to Cora's room. Part of her was afraid it would be blocked or guarded, but just like last night, the stairwell was empty. She raced up the stairs. For a moment, she paused outside the door before she opened it without knocking.

Light streamed in through the curtains and cut stripes of sunlight across the white bedding. Cora's eyes popped open as the door creaked. She didn't seem surprised to see her and watched her approach.

"Tell me about my mother." Her voice shook. She was certain whatever Cora hadn't told her last night would explain what was going on with her now. "There's something you're not telling me. I hurt Max just now when a bolt of energy came flying out of my hand." She held up her hand, wiggled her fingers and turned her hand this way and that way. "How was I able to do that? Why was I able to that? You said nothing about Oracles having those kinds of powers."

Cora patted the bed. "This is the first time they've manifested themselves, I take it?" The question seemed rhetorical since she didn't wait for an answer, but continued talking. "I wondered if they would manifest."

"What? Tell me what's happening to me." Her voice was bordering on shrill, but she didn't care. She wanted answers.

"Sit child and stop shrieking. I'll tell you."

Willow sat on the bed and held her tongue, afraid that if she said anything else, the woman might refuse to share.

"Hyacinth's visions and dreams became more prevalent a few years before she gave birth to you. Your mother knew she was different and that the things she saw weren't just random and meant nothing. She was seeing the future."

"When she saw your future, she knew the only way you stood a fighting chance was to make sure you could protect yourself... so she started to research to see if there were others like her. In her search she found out that witches, vampires and such weren't just make believe and fairytales. She infiltrated one of the supernatural hate groups to find out where she could find supernaturals, in particular faeries." Cora looked at her to gauge whether she understood. When Willow said nothing, she continued. "She waited until she was ovulating and went to a bar, slept with one of them and nine months later you were born. That's the story as she told it to me."

Slack jawed, Willow stared at Cora in shock. Her head was spinning. "My father's also a supernatural? She never talked about him... I just assumed she didn't want me to know him because he was a deadbeat... not this. Does he know about me?" It was hard to keep the hopefulness from her voice.

"I'm afraid not. During their evening together she found out he was a spiritual faery, but she said any information she told him was a fabrication so he could never figure out who she was or learn of you."

She deflated at that news. "So I guess that means she didn't get a last name."

Cora shook her head and grabbed her hand, a sympathetic look sat on her face. "You understand dear, that not only are you an Oracle, you're part fae."

Yeah, she was still processing that part too. Even if she wanted to figure out who her father was, she couldn't. She had no name, address, nothing. To him, it was just a drunken one-night stand. Her mother used him to get pregnant so she would be born with powers that would give her the ability to protect herself. He probably didn't remember her mother and since no one ever showed up on his doorstep in the last twenty-six years telling him he had a kid, he was more than likely living his best life.

"It's fine." She brushed it off and tried to appear unaffected. Opting instead to move onto a different round of questions. "Why faeries?" Willow wrinkled her nose in confusion. "Why not a witch or a shapeshifter? Don't they have more strength or powers or abilities than a faery?"

The old woman laughed a throaty laugh. "Child, you have much to learn."

Cora's knobby fingers patted her knee. "Your mother wanted to give you the best chance at survival. Being part fae gives you tremendous power. She knew you would go up against Killian and wanted you to rely on yourself."

"How did she find the coven? How did she get here?" Her brain and emotions still felt like they were spinning in a million different directions as she tried to wrap her mind around it all.

"She dreamed about it. In the dream she saw the face of the person who would lead her here. It was one of the Protectors. It didn't take her long to find him because she recognized the man as someone she bought her newspaper from every day."

Just like hers, her mother's Protectors had been hiding in plain sight, masquerading as friends, baristas and co-workers. "They don't interfere. It's part of the oath they take, but since your mother had full awareness of being the Oracle that went out the window." Cora coughed. "Water please." She wheezed out.

In her haste to get it, water sloshed over the edge of the pitcher when she grabbed it. After helping Cora take a few sips, the woman cleared her throat and reached over to her nightstand. A minute of fumbling around in the drawer produced whatever she was looking for. "She left this for you." Her knobby fingers deposited a videotape onto Willow's lap.

She picked it up and stared at it confused. "What am I supposed to do with this? It's a videotape. No one owns a VCR anymore."

Cora rolled her eyes, and the gesture made her appear fifty years younger.

"Dear, you're in a coven full of witches, someone should be able to rustle one up for you or locate one with a location spell. Plus, we collect things. I'm sure there's one in the attic or the cellar. Just have Eli get it for you." She yawned.

Willow knew their conversation was ending.

"Also, make sure he takes you to the library and gets books on faeries so you can understand the other half of your make-up." A bigger yawn followed. "Okay, now off with you dear. I'm tired." And just like that the old woman fell asleep before she could leave the room. Her snores followed her out the door.

When she turned, she found Eli waiting on the bench for her. He was still dressed in his sweats. "I thought I'd find you here." He stood and approached her.

"Is... is he okay?" Fear gripped her heart in its icy fingers. If she injured Max, she would never forgive herself.

"He's fine. Just a little dazed when he woke up, but he's okay."

The relief she felt was overwhelming. A breath she didn't realize she'd been holding whooshed out of her body.

She'd felt weighted down ever since she fled. Learning he would be okay made her lighter, like a balloon full of helium tethered to a piece of ribbon. She walked over and collapsed onto the bench he'd just left and dropped the tape on her lap. "That's good." She mumbled as she placed her head in her hands. Gratitude washed over her. The last thing she wanted was to worry about Max being hurt because of her. The roiling mass of thoughts that clogged her brain lessened.

"Is he mad at me? Is Phaedra?" She said through her fingers.

"No one is upset with you. Everyone knows it was an accident." He sat next to her. "Are you okay?"

She lifted her head and looked at him for several seconds before she shook it. "No."

"Want to talk about it?"

Their eyes stayed locked on one another. She shook her head again. It felt like she was unraveling. He was being so patient and understanding. "There is something you could help me with." She held up the videotape. "You wouldn't happen to have a VCR would you?"

"Let me just check my back pocket." He joked and pretended to reach for his pant's pocket.

Any other time she would have teased him for making a corny joke. Right now it coaxed a smile out of her and for that she was grateful.

He stood up and reached out his hand. "Come on. I think I can conjure us up a VCR." He smiled at her.

She returned his smiled and accepted his hand.

Back in the sitting room adjoining her bedroom, the flat screen TV Eli conjured looked out of place among the 18th century furnishings.

When he snapped his fingers and said the word, 'Appareo,' a cracking noise sounded right before the TV appeared. It impressed her.

"Did you just create that out of thin air?"

"No, when conjuring I have to know the object exists. It's easy with inanimate objects. It takes a lot of energy to conjure a person." He glanced at the television. "This TV came from my room. I thought about what I wanted and said the magic word. No pun intended. Let me see if I can recall where I saw a VCR. I believe there's one in Archie's room. Appareo." He snapped his fingers again, and the VCR appeared on the coffee table. Dust clung to the ancient electronic device.

"I'm not sure I remember how to operate one of these." It was heavier than she remembered she thought as she lifted the device to eye level to peer at it.

"Why don't I give you some privacy?" He got up to leave.

"Please don't go." She sat the VCR back down and stood.

He put his hands in his pockets and turned to her.

"My mother is on that tape and I don't think I want to watch it alone... please stay."

"Are you sure?"

She laughed nervously. "No."

He walked back and picked up the VCR. "Let's get this thing working." Eli's modern TV didn't have the proper connection needed for the older device so he pilfered the ancient TV that also belonged to Archie. With focus and concentration they had the older TV and VCR connected in ten minutes. She pushed in the videotape and took a seat beside him on the couch. His thigh brushed hers, but instead of the anxious stirrings of romance in her gut, she felt apprehension over what they would find on this tape.

Black-and-white striped vertical lines covered the screen. A few seconds later the picture kicked in and there on the screen was her mother.

"Mom." She scooted forward on the sofa and tried to swallow the lump of emotions that threatened to choke her. Unshed tears blinded her for a moment, but she blinked them away. Overwrought nerves made her grip the edge of the seat.

Her mother wore her long, natural curls loose and free. They rested just past her shoulders. A black, leather jacket covered her shoulders, which made her smile. It was the jacket she wore the day she left with the Protectors. It was one of the few possessions she had left that belonged to her mother. She refused to let them take it from her when she was sent to live in foster care.

"Is it on?" Her mother asked someone off-camera.

"Yes."

Her mom looked straight into the camera and smiled. "My sweet girl, if you're watching this it means..." Her smile faltered. "I was right and... and I'm dead."

Her breath hitched in her throat at her mother's statement. Even despite it being seventeen years since her mother died, it hurt to hear her say those words.

"I'm sorry I missed seeing you grow up. I'm sure you were strong and brave even without me, because that's what I taught you to be."

A single tear streamed down Willow's face and she swiped it away.

"There are things I need to tell you. A bad man named Killian will enter your dreams because he's trying to find you." Her mom moved closer to the screen like they were having a personal conversation. "Baby, I don't want you to be afraid. He'll be scary, but you'll be able to defeat him. I made sure that you're more than capable and powerful and you'll have help from the coven." She swallowed and looked at her lap. "I wish I had more time." Her mother was on the verge of tears. "Don't be frightened. I believe in you and I love you with all my heart." The video cut out and the screen cut to black and white fuzzy snow again.

They both just stared at the screen.

"What did she mean by, 'She made sure you were more than capable and powerful?' Does that have anything to do with what happened today?"

His eyes searched her face for answers. So much had changed in her life already, the last thing she wanted was for him to change towards her once she told him, but she couldn't keep it a secret. Turning towards him, she met his gaze. There was a part of her that wanted to look away. Instead, she stared back unflinching. "I'm half fae." Tension filled the air as she waited to see what he would say. His face was a blank mask before he spoke.

"That explains a lot. How you could get in my head that day..." He looked at her hands, balled into fists on her lap. "It explains how you could shoot blasts of energy from your hands." His eyes met her eyes again, and he smiled. "Looks like we have some new training to do."

His response allowed her to relax. She uncurled her fists and grinned back at him. A warm feeling curled around her like a blanket. She was glad she asked him to stay. They were sitting so close. If wishes became reality, he'd put his arms around her and hold her, but knew that wouldn't happen. Anytime she attempted to get closer he backed off and got skittish. He just wasn't into her. She wished she didn't find him so damned attractive. Every time they were alone, or he looked at her like he was looking at her now, she wished he would kiss her. She pushed her disappointment aside. "Thanks for making all of this easier."

CHAPTER 20

Eli

WILLOW WAS HALF-FAE. An Oracle had never mated with another supernatural before, only a human. After they watched the tape, she relayed the story her mother told Cora. Hyacinth wanted her daughter to be prepared for the battle ahead and had done the only thing she knew to help keep her safe. She'd armed her with more powers. The woman was cunning. He'd give her that.

The others poured over spell books and mixed brews in their cauldrons. They'd be back on the road soon and everyone wanted to have potions ready for any further ambushes. He glanced at his watch again. The door opened, and he looked up.

"Sorry, I got lost." Willow stood in the doorway.

"It's okay." He walked towards her.

"We aren't doing combat training today?" She glanced at her workout attire and then towards everyone working diligently.

"Thought you and I could take a trip to the coven's library and research..." He let his statement hang in the air.

"Do they know?" She whispered to him, but her eyes darted to the others.

"I figured you'd tell them when you're ready, but I have to say the sooner you do the better."

They were interrupted when Max walked into the room behind them. At his arrival, her demeanor changed. "I guess today is as good a day as any." She looked him in the eye. "I owe Max an apology for what happened." She stepped away from him and raised her voice so she could be heard. "I have something I need to tell all of you."

The chopping, mixing and measuring stopped and everyone gave her their undivided attention. She pressed her fist into her palm and looked out at their expectant faces. "I learned yesterday that..." Her eyes found his, and he nodded to encourage her to continue. "I learned that I'm part faery." She turned to Max. "That's how I could shoot that blast of energy from my fist... I'm sorry I hurt you. I didn't mean to."

Max's face was unreadable as he approached her. It was noticeable Willow wanted to take a step back, but she stood her ground. He stopped in front of her and said nothing for several seconds before he broke into a huge grin and chuckled. "Of course I forgive you. I know it wasn't intentional. You don't spend seven years with someone and not know what kind of person they are. Come here." He hugged. "So part faery huh?" He pulled back and looked at her. "So when do you grow wings?"

Laughter sounded around the room as she playfully swatted him.

"That's actually where I was going to take Willow this morning, to the library so we can do some research. I don't think she'll be sprouting wings anytime soon, Max."

"This is so cool. I haven't gotten to meet any faeries before." Mathilda's girlish glee was infectious. The others wore bright smiles too.

He knew the rest of them had had encounters with faeries. It was always a mixed bag when dealing with them. You never knew what kind you would get since there were so many varieties and species. Willow may never know exactly what kind of faery she was, but he would do everything in his power to help her learn her abilities. "We'll join you guys for combat training later this evening." He motioned for her to follow him out into the hallway. When he looked up, he didn't miss the look that Phaedra was giving him. He averted his gaze. Yes, he would be alone with her, but it was so he could help her research and study, nothing more. Nothing would happen. He tried not to scowl once they left the room.

"Thank you so much. Cora told me to ask you to help me so I appreciate that now it doesn't feel like I'm burdening you since you suggested it first." Her rambling made him glance at her. Was she nervous?

"I would help you. It's my duty."

Her footsteps faltered, and he turned to look at her. She gave him a lackluster smile before looking at the floor. Had he done something wrong? The thought plagued him on the way to the library.

The room was crammed to the rafters with books. They spilled from shelves and some even sat piled on the floor. Rows of books filled the room with a few tables and chairs scattered about. A stooped over old woman came forward when they entered. A smile tugged at the corners of his mouth when he saw her. The woman looked frail, but her grip was strong as she pulled him down for a hug.

"This is Enid. Keeper of Books."

"Silly boy." She chuckled and released him.

Willow held out her hand, but the woman batted it away and hugged her.

"She is Archie's twin sister and the librarian for the coven. Any book we need, she'll find it."

"You flatter me too much." Despite what she said, she preened like a peacock at his words.

Once they were seated at a table, he rubbed his hands together and addressed Enid.

"We're looking for books about faeries. Books that detail their abilities, history, anything you got." He gave her the information like he was ordering from a restaurant menu.

She closed her eyes and raised her hands into the air. "Books hear my voice and come when I call. Bring me books, poems, fairytales, histories, manuals and everything about faeries. Veniunt ad me." When she opened her eyes books came flying off the shelves and began to stack themselves into piles on the table where they sat.

"What does that mean?" She whispered while her eyes watched the books that floated and whizzed through the air.

"Most of our spells, chants and incantations use Latin. 'Veniunt ad me,' means come to me now."

She merely nodded her head at his explanation and continued to watch in fascination.

It was hard not to feel the shock, surprise and awe that Willow felt as she watched Enid work. Her mouth hung open and her eyes were round with wonder. When it was over she turned to Eli, her face beaming. "Oh, my goodness. That was like being in a Disney movie." The level of childlike excitement must have embarrassed her because she dialed it back before speaking again. "Very few things used to surprise me, but... ever since I met you, I mean ever since you talked to me," This statement made them both laugh. "I'm surprised ten times a day."

He tried to deflect. "It has nothing to do with me and everything to do with you finding out about supernaturals." It was bad enough they were alone. The last thing he wanted was her attributing any special feelings to him. One title caught his eye, and he grabbed the book. "Let's get started."

While they worked he overheard her hum a tune and realized it was The Cure's 'Lovesong' that they'd heard on the radio on the way to the coven. He cleared his throat and tried to block it out. Even humming, her voice sounded amazing. It could easily lull him into doing something he shouldn't. Like finding some place cozy in the book stacks and kissing her senseless. He shook himself.

No.

"You should look at this." He reached the book across the table while discreetly adjusting the hard-on that was growing in his pants. If he engaged her, then she would stop singing and he wouldn't feel so turned on by her. Willow took it from him and flipped through the pages. He was both happy and disappointed when her humming stopped.

"Did you know that spiritual faeries have more powerful abilities than physical faeries? They're only surpassed by ethereal faeries." She sounded proud of her newfound lineage.

"I wasn't aware of that."

"Do you think I'll be able to do this?" Enthusiasm seeped from her pores while her index finger pointed at an illustration in the book.

Stupidly, he came around the table to stand next to her so he could see. Peering over her shoulder and being this close to her made his body respond in a way it shouldn't. The picture showed an image of a faery entering another person's body. Possession. Or maybe it was astral projection. Either way, both were difficult.

"It's a possibility that's a power you possess, but it could take time to get you there if you have it. Possession isn't an easy thing to do. Astral projection is even harder. Plus, you're half fae. Sometimes that limits the abilities you inherit."

Her face dropped.

"I'm not trying to discourage you. I just don't want you to think you can jump into bodies right away... that's all." He amended his earlier statement trying to infuse humor. "The more I can get you in tune with your inner mind," Gently, he pressed his forefinger and middle finger to the center of her forehead, "the easier manifesting your powers and abilities will be."

They spent the rest of the morning going through the myriad of books that Enid had found for them. The way she laughed at a book of faery limericks, with her head tossed back, eyes closed and her hand over her belly, made him want to keep finding ways to making her laugh.

"There once was a faery from Derry;

Who always was quite very merry.

He liked to drink,

But not to think

So he often found himself in a quandary."

Some books unearthed more serious content about the numerous abilities and powers that faeries could have. Other tomes spoke of the history of faeries among humans and other supernaturals. All of it fascinated her. It was hard to pull his eyes away from her as she poured over every book soaking up the knowledge with a newfound sense of wonder.

After they exhausted themselves with reading he dragged her back to the makeshift gym for more training. On the way there she asked him about the house. "This house is pretty old, huh?"

"Yeah it was built in the early 1600s." He stopped walking and turned to her. "During the Salem Witch Trials they used it as a safe haven to harbor witches that fled persecution and the threat of being imprisoned or executed." He enjoyed feeding her thirst for knowledge since she'd stepped into the supernatural world.

"Like an underground railroad, but for witches?"

He nodded in agreement to her comparison. "Yes, very similar."

Most of the others had already left by the time they returned. The rest he shooed from the room.

"Don't we kind of need them if I'm going to spar with someone?"

He shut the door on Zoriana. Thankful that Phaedra wasn't one of the people he'd just kicked out or he would never hear the end of it. "Instead of jumping back into combat training we need to work on tapping into your powers." The look he saw on her face was not what he expected. "I thought you'd jump at the chance to work on figuring out your abilities." He approached her.

"It's just..." She rocked back on her heels while eyeing the ground. "You saw how well it went the first time. I don't think I'm any good at this."

Before he knew what he was doing, he grabbed her by the shoulders. "Don't underestimate yourself. This is all new. No one expects you to get it right away..." Her eyes found his. "Don't be so hard on yourself. Okay?" He dropped his hands and took a step back.

What does she use in her hair?

He had to stop getting so close. Her smell was intoxicating. Whatever body wash or shampoo she used made him want to lick her, taste her. He took a deep breath. "Let's begin."

Moments later, she sat in front of him cross-legged with her hands resting on her knees, palms facing upwards. An unsure look marked her face. She had yet to close her eyes, but she wouldn't look at him.

"Do you trust me?"

His question must have startled her because her eyes flew up from her lap to meet his. "Do you trust me?" He repeated.

Several seconds passed before she answered him. "Well, I have worked with you for over a year where you never spoke to me and then one day I woke up in your bed, where you told me I had magical psychic powers." She folded her arms across her chest. "Let's see. Then I went on the run with you and an RV full of witches and a werewolf that used to be my dog. I was attacked and now I'm here at your coven." A smirk lit up her face. "I think the answer to your question is obvious."

His lip twitched as he tried to suppress a grin. "A yes would have sufficed."

"Where's the fun in that?" Her smirk turned into an impish grin and there was a part of him that wanted to kiss the cute look right off her face. He cleared his throat and copied her earlier position with his hands resting on his legs palms facing upward.

"Back into position and close your eyes." He made his voice sound more gruff and authoritative so he wouldn't think about having her beneath him on the mat.

She obeyed.

"We've done this part before. Clear your mind. Empty it of everything, past, present..." He watched her breathing even out. "That's good." A few minutes passed without him saying a word. He wanted her to focus on her breathing and clearing her mind. "Everything you are is already inside of you, Willow... all you have to do is tap into it. Tap into your inner mind and your gifts will manifest themselves."

She breathed deeply, but he could tell she was struggling. It was going to be a long night.

CHAPTER 21

Willow

THE LAST COUPLE weeks passed in a blur of trainings, day in and day out. She'd only had two migraines since arriving. Could that be attributed to staying at the coven? Morgana was kind enough to sit with her during one of the episodes. During that episode she dreamed of Killian. It was nice to wake up from the nightmare and not find herself alone. She was grateful to Morgana for being there.

Alternating between various combat trainings, studying in the library and meditation had her exhausted. Plus, she didn't feel like she was making as much progress as she should be. Her combat skills had definitely improved, but the supernatural abilities were a different story.

Eli was very pleased, but she expected more. She was getting the hang of using the energy blasts and learning how to control them during combat. There had only been one other incident. When she meditated, she would see flashes of the future like she had the first time. They came so quick. She still wasn't able to identify what she was seeing. Some of her other faery powers were making appearances, but at the most awkward and inappropriate times.

In the shower, a few days ago she created faery dust out of nowhere and ended up covering herself and the shower in the magical, glittery, powder. Not all the dust would wash out of her hair, so she walked around with shimmery hair the rest of the day, which resulted in everyone calling her Tinker Bell.

The dust eventually faded she realized as she wiped the steam from the mirror after her shower. "Finally." She muttered to herself while finger combing through her hair. Her muscles were sore from the earlier combat session. She rubbed them through the fluffy bathrobe and walked into her bedroom. Sleep was pulling and tugging at every part of her physically and mentally. The long yawn that left her mouth made her shake her head. The minute she hit the mattress she was asleep in seconds.

Where am I?

When the thought entered her mind she knew she was dreaming, but wherever she was, she'd never been there before. She looked down at her body and saw she was still wearing the bathrobe. A chill crept up her spine because this felt eerily real. In any other dream she wore a random outfit. The hallway was massive, like she was in a palace. Her bare feet made no sound as she tiptoed down the corridor, frightened she would encounter someone. This place had an ominous feeling. She shouldn't be here.

"Wake up. Wake up. Wake up." The whispered words did nothing, because she remained in the dream or whatever it was.

A large doorway loomed at the end of the hall. The door was slightly ajar. Against her better judgment she crept towards it.

What am I doing? Why am I going to investigate? I should head in the other direction.

Despite the screaming thoughts in her brain she proceeded to the door, frantically looking around for anyone or anything that might lurk in the shadows. The sliver of an opening was enough for her to press her eye to and attempt to look around without being caught. It was a bedroom. There were floor to ceiling windows on the far side of the room. There must have been a balcony or terrace situated outside because the flimsy, gauzy curtains billowed out from the windows, caught by a breeze. In the dimness she could barely make out a sleeping form in the cavernous bed. The room seemed devoid of anything else, save a large armoire.

Something made her crack the door open and walk inside.

What are you doing you crazy person? Go back. Get out of here.

Still she moved closer, her curiosity carrying her closer and closer. Seconds later, she stood on the stairs that led up to the bed. Her hand and arm shook as she reached out to touch the shoulder of the sleeping form that had their back to her.

"Who's there?"

His sinister voice froze her in place. The hairs all over her body stood on end. This was Killian's bedroom. He rolled over and sat up. The covers slipped down revealing his naked chest. His green eyes scanned the darkened chamber. She was sure his vampire sight allowed him to see just fine despite the lack of light. The crazy thing was, he seemed to look right through her like she wasn't even there. She waved her hand in front of his face.

"You can't see me?"

His eyes continued to search the room. While she was definitely dumbstruck that she was invisible to him, her mind chose that moment to have a stupid thought.

If he's a vampire why isn't he sleeping in a coffin or underground?

She wanted to kick herself.

Really? Right now is not the time for this.

"I can smell the witch on you, Willow." His nostrils flared.

Her body went rigid with terror.

He knows I'm here.

The derision in his statement made her wonder if he knew she was staying at the Walker Coven. After the attack he already knew she traveled with witches.

"I will find you." He sounded so sure she swallowed to keep from choking and clutched her throat feeling like he was strangling her.

Wake up!

Her eyes flew open, and she took in a deep, much needed breath before she sat up and looked around the beige and white, eighteenth century bedroom she occupied at the coven and sighed.

***

The next morning she was in the library bright and early. She hadn't expected to find Enid there already, but there she was. The old woman gave her some space and Willow claimed the table she and Eli had occupied before and poured over some books that discussed faery powers. That had been no ordinary dream last night. She'd never been able to do that before. How had she placed herself in Killian's bedroom? There had to be an explanation.

Two hours later, that's where Eli found her, surrounded by faery books hungrily gobbling up every crumb of faery knowledge she could.

"You were supposed to meet me for training."

Wrangling the snarkiness she wanted to spew at that moment, she took the high road and ignored the annoyance in his voice. "I know. I know, but something happened last night."

Eli dropped into the seat across from her. "I'm listening."

She pushed the book she'd been browsing away from her and rested her folded arms on the table. "Last night, I dreamed about Killian."

The chair scraped against the wooden floorboards when he jerked to the edge of his seat. "What? Why didn't you come to me right away?"

This time she didn't bother to hide the eye rolling. "I know you're one of my Protectors, but I'm not always going to come running to you for everything."

If he planned to say anything in return, he chose not to. His face was a blank mask.

It hadn't been her intention to hurt his feelings. She needed him to know she could take care of herself. History may have painted Oracles as some damsels in distress, but that was no longer the case. She pulled the book back towards her. "The dream I had wasn't like the other dreams. I didn't have a headache before dreaming about him. I came here this morning because one power I've read about that faeries have is this." She slid the book towards him.

"Dream manipulation." He read aloud and then looked back at her.

"I think I was in his dream last night and not him in mine." At his look of confusion she kept talking. "I wish I could explain it better, but I can't. I just know it wasn't like all the other dreams." She sighed and leaned back in her chair. She picked at something beneath her thumbnail in frustration. "He knew I was there, even though he couldn't see me."

While she pretended to find more interest in her nails, she noticed him lean his elbows on the table. "What do you mean he couldn't see you?" The patience he exhibited while he waited for her to respond was impressive.

She dug at her nail a few seconds longer before she responded. "I was invisible to him. Before you even ask, I'm not sure how I did it. I wasn't even aware that I was invisible until he woke up and caught me." Leaning on the table, she finally looked at him. "Listen, can we just go meditate and train? I really want to nail this and I'm not going to do that by talking it to death. I will master it by doing it. You said you're here to help me, so help me." She expelled a quick breath.

For a few seconds he stared at her. Neither his face nor body conveyed emotion. "Okay, let's go train." His mouth lifted in a lopsided grin.

***

The only phrase that came to mind hours later as she sat cross-legged on the floor in the training room where they'd locked themselves away was: *Be careful what you wish for.*

"Stop telling me what you can't do and just do it. You said you wanted this so I'm going to keep pushing you."

The mental energy she'd been exerting had left her body spent. Sweat poured out of every pore like she'd been doing hot yoga.

He walked around her. "Let's go again." They'd started off with him seated in front of her, but as the session wore on he'd gotten up and paced circles around her; being a hard to please taskmaster, issuing order after order. When she didn't shut her eyes right away to try again, he barked at her. "Again"

"I can't." She could feel how close she was to attaining what she wanted, but her brain was feeling like a sizzling egg on a skillet. Anymore mental gymnastics and she would vomit, pass out or both. She was about to stand up when he placed his hands on her shoulders preventing her from getting up. His eyes met hers.

"You can. Now try harder." This time he said the words softer and with even more conviction. "Push past whatever mental block is in your way. You can do this. I know you can."

In his eyes, shone the complete faith he had in her. Seeing his belief written there so plainly gave her the courage and renewed strength to keep pushing. She shut her eyes and cleared her mind of everything like a teacher erasing answers on a chalkboard; it was all wiped away: whatever happened today, the nightmares, the things she learned about her mother, the music career she would never have. It was a clean white space by the time she finished. She heard his voice from afar off. "Tap into who you are Willow. You're the Oracle."

Something occurred that had not before. An inner voice spoke.

'Show me.'

After the voice spoke, her eyes flew open, and she fell into a trance. The flood of imagery that usually rushed through her mind slowed down and became mini silent films in her mind. There were some images she still couldn't make sense of their purpose because there wasn't enough context: images of Phaedra yelling at Samson, the dagger that Eli had given her, an unkempt Eli with a full beard weeping, a female hand not touched by age resting on a large leather-bound book that appeared ancient, and her standing in front of Killian with a hooded figure standing behind him in the background. One image that stuck out in her mind was of her kissing a very willing and enthusiastic Eli. The images cut off, and she blinked.

"Willow?" His troubled look eased some when she met his eyes. "Your eyes turned a milky white when you..." His voice drifted off and he stared at her. "That didn't happen last time."

"I believe it's because I saw the future this time... well snippets of the future." The trembling in her body should have been because of the images of impending doom, instead the single image of her in a heated lip lock with Eli was what caused palpitations. She couldn't stop staring at him.

"You've had flashes before..."

"This was different." Her eyes raked over his face. "They were slower. Like home movies, but not grainy or anything. They were coming in like HD clear."

"That's great, Willow. You did it. I told you, you could do it."

Before she could react, he pulled her into a tight hug. It was surreal.

"Come have dinner with me." He pulled away from her with a joyous expression and looked at her.

"What?" She felt breathless as she looked at him stunned. Did he just ask her out on a date? Maybe he said it in the heat of the moment. They were both on a high from her being able to recall the future images that had come across in her mind. Could the image she saw be true? Her heart sped up at the thought.

"My mother's been dying to meet you and it's our last night here. Come to dinner and meet my parents. We can celebrate."

Wasn't meeting the parents something that came much later? She'd never progressed to that point in a relationship where anyone had wanted her to meet their parents.

"You must still be in shock from whatever you saw for it to leave you speechless. Let's have dinner and then you can tell me about it later tonight." He stood.

All she could do was nod like a bobble head. He reached his hand out to help her up, and she took it and let him pull her to her feet.

"We both stink." Broken out of her dazed state, she laughed. He grinned.

"Lets both shower and change and I'll pick you up from your room for dinner."

She looked away, trying to hide the flush that crept across her face at the mention of showering. It was obvious he meant separately, but since seeing the kiss, her mind was turning everything into dirty innuendo.

CHAPTER 22

Eli

IT WAS SHOCKING to find the rest of the Protectors dressed up and seated at the table when they arrived. He'd been unsure whether it was his mother or father's doing. Not that this was a date or anything. Between Phaedra and his father, he wasn't sure who had sent him more disparaging looks. He avoided them throughout the meal and focused on the other conversations happening at the table, but he hadn't been able to stop himself from looking at Willow time and time again.

The taste of the food had yet to register in his brain. He sat across from her and all he could think about was when she opened the door earlier this evening. He'd never seen her look lovelier. The short, sleeveless, diaphanous, pale pink dress gave her the magical appearance of a faery. It was moments like this that had his years of training and discipline taking a backseat to his heart that frightened him. He swallowed down the mass of food that sat in his mouth and tuned in to listen to Mathilda's excited banter.

"And then I mixed more sage and thistle root to the brew instead of burdock root and I was able to create the potion to the exact specifications I needed." Mathilda concluded her tale of potion mixing. His mother had sat her and Zoriana next to each other, but it was clear the chasm between them still hadn't been breached. Mathilda told him she would try to mend things. It hadn't happened, or it didn't work. He wasn't sure which.

"She's a natural." Morgana rubbed her back while she praised her. A quick glance at Zoriana revealed a hurt look she quickly tried to mask. Her eyes dropped to the table, and she took a small bite of her food. The chatter resumed, and he resolved that he would make them sit in a room together until they fixed what was between them.

"Everything's delicious." Vigorous nods, murmurs of agreement and sounds of forks scraping nearly empty plates followed Max's compliment.

"More broccoli, dear? It's great brain food and I've heard how hard you've been working." His mother beamed at Willow while she offered the green vegetable from the platter that hovered in the air near her.

"Thank you." She graciously accepted more.

"You're leaving here tomorrow. Is there a plan?" The question from his father brought everything to a grinding halt. Leave it to him to ruin the mood and cross-examine him in front of everyone.

"Well, we would never stay here at the coven indefinitely. It's only a matter of time before Killian knows exactly who she is, if he doesn't already. I won't endanger the people here by staying. We have to keep moving." His mouth tightened at being second-guessed over his leadership skills. The cool water glass he reached for helped to quell some of his growing anger once he took a sip.

"That's fine, but..." His father's attempt to keep the interrogation going at the dinner table in front of everyone had him gripping the glass tighter. If it shattered into shards in his hand, he'd welcome the pain of the jagged glass in his palm if it stopped the anger that was quickly boiling over to the point of eruption.

"I know whatever Eli has planned will keep us all safe."

His head whipped towards Willow.

"I trust him completely." She stared back at him with an amount of surety in his ability he didn't expect to see there. Even though she had no idea how deep and twisted the roots ran on the dysfunction of his relationship with his father or the role she played in their growing animosity, he was grateful to her for standing up for him.

'THANK YOU.' He delivered his gratitude through their mind link. She looked up and gifted him with a small smile.

There was no time to ponder or linger over her coming to his rescue because he knew without looking at his father what kind of expression he would find on his face after hearing Willow interject on his behalf. His father disapproved of him training her alone. He didn't trust that Eli would stay true to the Protector's commandment and not become romantically involved with her.

Phaedra came to the rescue before anything could get out of hand. "Eli knows the more he trains Willow her visions will grow stronger and eventually give us insight into how to defeat Killian. Until then, we must keep moving so it is harder for him to find her. There is a method to the madness."

Eli gave her an imperceptible nod of thanks and she returned it with a look of 'I got you.' He was always thankful to have her in his corner. His father respected her opinion. This time was no different. He resumed eating his food and the talk at the table returned to mundane things.

The rest of the meal passed without a repeat inquisition from his father. At the end of the dinner party, he said his goodbyes to his parents knowing they would get on the road first thing in the morning. He reminded everyone to be at the RV bright and early ready to pack up and move on. Afterward he escorted Willow to her room.

"Do you want to come in?"

He stuffed his hand into his pocket and rubbed the back of his neck with the other. "Um."

"Just for a little while?" The soft feminine plea so unlike her, made him cave.

"Sure."

She closed the door once he stepped inside. Awkwardness ensued as they fidgeted and looked anywhere, but at each other.

"There's a bar. Did you want a nightcap?" She walked across the room to the sideboard that hid a stash of various liquors. Her nimble fingers made quick work of filling two tumblers with a smoky, amber colored liquid. When she walked back and placed the glass in his hands she stood close. As she tipped the glass back and drank down the fiery beverage, his eyes were riveted on her. She winced. "That's stronger than I thought." A cough and a small giggle followed that teased of flirtation.

The smile she wore was not the smile of a woman skilled in the art of seduction, but that of an innocent girl, newly ripe for romance. He had a hard time not smiling back. Although his smile felt more like a grimace you gave when you'd eaten something bad, but you were trying hard to act like you were unaffected. He had yet to take a sip of alcohol. If he was honest, he was feeling a bit intoxicated already. It was probably because of their proximity or her body language cues he was sure he was not misreading.

"Maybe I should let you get some sleep, since we have an early day tomorrow." The glass landed on the coffee table a little harder than he planned in his clumsy haste to get out of there. He'd nearly reached the door when her voice stopped him.

"Wait." Some unseen force anchored him to the ground at that one word. He couldn't leave. When he turned back, she had closed the distance between them. "Don't go."

In her eyes, he saw the unspoken emotions that lay between them. He didn't want to put a name to any of it, because he had been trying so hard not to lay claim to any of the strong feelings he felt himself. She was about to say something.

"Don't Willow." He could use his magic to will her to stay silent and not do or say whatever she was about to do, but the idea died just as quickly as it sprung up in his mind. She placed her hand over his mouth and the scent of jasmine and lavender from whatever lotion she used earlier wafted up his nostrils.

"I need to say this to you, Eli, even though I'm nervous and scared as hell."

She was standing so close to him that as he stared at her, for the first time, he noticed there were tiny golden flecks in the browns of her eyes.

"Ever since I first saw you at the office, I was attracted to you. When you didn't speak to me that day I was hurt...

so when I found out everything and learned that you were only being rude because you didn't want me to find out you were a witch and my protector," She gave another nervous giggle, "You know that whole story... anyway, since then, my feelings have grown stronger for you. And before you say anything, it's not because you've been protecting me, because honestly sometimes you've been an ass to me..."

Any other day, her frankness might have made him chuckle, right now his arms hung limply at his sides and he felt like a stunned bird that had made the mistake of flying into a window.

"What I'm trying to say is..." She expelled a breath and with her heart shining in her eyes professed the way she felt like she was a death row inmate making her final plea on execution day. "I think I'm in love with you." In a gesture he assumed allowed him to speak, she removed her hand from his mouth, but before he could say anything she kissed him. It was the kind of kiss that stole your breath, stopped your heart, but then in a split second resuscitated you and brought you back to life, made you realize how sweet life could be.

Before he could stop himself his arms wound themselves around her lower back and waist and he pulled her closer, his lips clamored for more of the taste of her. Her body was soft in all the right places. He savored the taste of brandy that lingered on her tongue and lips when he sucked her succulent bottom lip into his mouth. A small moan of pleasure escaped her and he hardened at the sound and pressed his erection against her.

Her response spurred him on and he deepened the kiss. It was surprising when she allowed him to take the lead. With all the sparring and back and forth they'd had in their interactions with one another he'd assumed he'd have to bend her to his will. He thoroughly enjoyed her sweetness, but if he was honest with himself, he enjoyed her strong-willed nature and wanted the same in a sexual relationship. His teeth nipped at her bottom lip and he felt her smile against his mouth. He knew that smile. It was a smile that said, 'I'm a little kinky, but I wasn't sure you were.' When she sank her teeth into his bottom lip, he let out a groan of pleasure. She licked the indentation of her teeth marks to take away the sweet sting, before their tongues dueled for dominance and he found it sexy as hell.

She was walking backwards and pulling him towards the sofa when reality finally crash-landed in his brain. He wasn't supposed to be kissing her. It was forbidden. His father would relish the thought of him not being able to honor the code he'd sworn to when he became a Protector. As much as he wanted her, he couldn't go through with this.

Instinctively, he pulled back from her. Her eyes were still clouded with lust as she reached for him, her lips puckered, bee stung and ready for another make-out session. Gripping her hands between his own, he panted. "I can't." He took a few staggering steps away from her. If he didn't put some distance between them, he would take her in his arms again and next time he wouldn't stop. He'd brand every inch of her flesh with his mouth and tongue before making her body his. It cut him to the quick to see the varying emotions transform her face from confused to embarrassed and eventually to wounded once realization set in that he was rejecting her.

"I don't understand." Her slender fingers rubbed her lips before touching her cheek. She stepped towards him like her invasion of his personal space would entice him to continue or change his mind. In the next instant, her eyes widened and her mouth opened slightly before her mouth snapped shut and tightened into a grim line. She dropped her eyes to the floor and took a step back, wrapping her arms around herself.

Even though she no longer looked at him, he could see her watery eyes trying to withstand her broken heart. It made him sick to his stomach she had unpacked her feelings like a long-time traveler that had finally found somewhere to call home; only to be told there was no vacancy. Revealed what lay in her heart and laid it at his feet and he'd stepped on it and crushed it and ground it into dust. He swallowed and tried to find the words to repair what he'd broken. "Willow, I..."

"Just go." The anguished tremor her voice became continued to tear out his guts. On the slow walk to the door, he thought about casting a spell to reverse time and take him back to just before she invited him inside for a nightcap. He could politely decline and never have to hurt her. He held the door open unable to walk through just yet. One more glance back showed a single tear running down her cheek. "I'm sorry." It was pathetic and lame, and the only words he could manage.

"Go!" The ragged sob ripped itself from her throat and she turned her back.

He knew it was wrong and unfair of him to linger and attempt to plead his case any further. She was hurting and angry and she deserved to be left alone. Once the door closed, and he stood on the other side, he heard the soul-crushing wail she'd stifled before he walked out. He pressed his forehead and palm against the door. It took every fiber of his being not to race back inside and try to comfort her, but he was the last person she wanted to see at this moment.

CHAPTER 23

Willow

SHE'D NEVER BEEN the woman that cried over men, but the tear stains covering her pillow showed otherwise. When he rebuffed her before with his chilly reception at the office that day she'd been able to deal. She had her crummy job, an aspiring music career, her dog and a few friendly colleagues she hung with. Right now it felt like she had nothing. Her music career would never happen. She wasn't sure she'd ever be able to go home again. Essentially, she was a vagabond, tooling around with a group of virtual strangers. She didn't even have her dog anymore. Plus, it seemed like she would never master powers that were supposed to be her birthright.

And now someone that could be one of the few good things in her life rejected her... again. Maybe it wouldn't hurt so much if she hadn't grown so close to him over the last couple months. After her mother died, and they moved her to a new state she found it hard to make friends. When you were someone who grew up having no best friends, and you finally made a connection with someone, it hurt deeply when it was ripped away. Not only had he broken her heart last night, she felt like she'd lost a good friend. How could things ever go back to what they had before this happened? It was impossible.

When she dragged herself under the hot spray of the showerhead, she hoped the water would soothe her, but it didn't. Her heart still ached and bled with pain. Why had the vision shown him kissing her, if he was only going to reject her? Confusion twisted itself into knotted balls of yarn inside her head. She needed to understand more about how her visions worked. Was it just glimmers of events? Could things be altered or changed? Were they just possibilities that held various outcomes?

When she stepped from the shower, someone was knocking on her door. The fluffy bathrobe that lay nearby covered her wet nakedness before she padded to the door in bare feet. She answered without a greeting and found Mathilda waiting there. It was hard trying to push through her heartache and offer a false smile.

"You okay?" Mathilda looked at her with deep concern.

"I'm fine." She shifted her gaze, attempting to hide her red-rimmed eyes. The protruding design of the doorknob would leave an imprint in her palm she gripped it so tightly. She pushed the door slightly to hide more of herself. "Did you want something?" She didn't mean to sound so cold to the girl, but if Eli had sent her to convey some message, she didn't want to hear it.

Mathilda's eyes widened in shock at her tone. "Um... Cora wanted to see you before we left."

Before she could try to apologize for her mood Mathilda scurried off.

Damn it!

Clutching the folds of her robe, she stepped into the hall ready to call her back, but said nothing. It was clear, whatever she said at that moment might only make things worse. Just because she got her feelings stomped on last night, did not give her the right to terrorize someone else. Mathilda had been nothing but nice since all of this happened. The spunky teenager was like a younger sister to her. She needed to find her and apologize for her behavior. While she dressed she got herself in the right headspace with a firm talking to. She promised herself she wouldn't dish out boatloads of attitude and misery to everyone that crossed her path. There was only one person who had earned her anger.

After dressing in a black tank top, black skinny jeans and knee high black boots she grabbed her leather jacket before leaving the room to visit Cora. With no one's aid she was glad she only got lost once on the way. It had been some time since her last visit. She peered into the old woman's room before stepping inside. "Cora?"

"I'm awake." Her voice croaked. "Come in, come in." As usual, she sat propped against the pillows, looking like she was holding court from bed. Willow wondered if there was a nurse or caretaker that scuttled out of sight when she received visitors. Or did they vanish? After all, this was a witch house. It's not like they had to use doors. She pushed the thought away and sat on the edge of the bed.

"There was something I didn't give you when you visited last time." Her fingers patted some papers.

How had she not noticed them before? A tidy bundle of letters wrapped up in ribbon rested on Cora's lap.

"These are letters your mother wrote to you."

"Why didn't you just give them to me when you gave me the videotape?" Her eyes narrowed in suspicion. What game was she playing at withholding the letters?

A cunning, crafty smile of a con artist that's just revealed you didn't select the money card in a game of Three-card Monte crossed Cora's face. "Sometimes things need to come in steps and stages of what we can handle and how soon we can handle it." She held out the pile of letters with both hands. "You're ready for these."

"You seem to have a flair for the dramatic, old woman." Willow accepted the letters, unable to hide the slight grin that flitted across her face.

Cora squinted and leaned forward, her eyes drawn to her necklace. She reached out and traced the snake pendant that dangled from the chain. The curious faraway look in her gaze had Willow wondering about her thoughts. "What is it?" When Cora pulled her hand away, she grabbed the snake between her forefinger and thumb and rubbed it.

"Where did you get that?" Cora's eyes darted to hers after she ripped them from the necklace.

"My mother gave it to me." She knew there was something behind the question. "Why?"

Cora's eyes went back to the necklace once more, but she said nothing. Her eyes probed the old woman's face for any acknowledgement, but she got nothing.

"I'm tired." Her shoulders slumped against the pillows and she closed her eyes. Thin blue veins could be seen in the translucent skin of her eyelids. Part of her believed this was just a ploy to get rid of her. Several minutes passed without the woman opening her eyes or acknowledging her presence. There was nothing more she would get from her. She took the letters and headed for the door. Before she could step outside, Cora spoke. "Take care, child."

Willow looked back towards the bed, but Cora still lay in the same position with her eyes shut. She closed the door and left, wondering if she'd ever cross paths with the old woman again.

Back in her room, she finished packing up and stuffed the weathered envelopes into her bag. She donned her mother's aged leather jacket. Something felt different. After spending time at the coven, wearing the jacket felt like she was being wrapped in the warm embrace of her mother's arms. Even though her mother's scent no longer lingered in the jacket's folds, she couldn't help pressing the sleeve to her nose and inhaling.

One of the last pieces she needed to pack sat on the bed. The dagger she'd so loved in Samson's store that Eli gifted her with as a surprise lay beside her bag. She was of half a mind to ditch it, but the beautiful blade made her smile every time she saw it. Plus, she'd admired it and wanted it before Eli gave it to her. She wouldn't be keeping it because it was from him, but because she had always liked it. Pulling the dagger from the sheath, her finger ran along the cold steel. No, she'd hang onto it, even though he gave it to her. She shoved it into her bag next to the letters.

Outside, her jaw fell open when instead of the old 1970s RV they'd been riding through the countryside in, she saw a sleek, state-of-the-art mobile home that probably was even more geeked out on the inside. Her sadness was momentarily forgotten when Max walked up dressed like Spicoli from *Fast Times At Ridgemont High*. "Isn't it awesome? Morgana got permission from the Council to give us an upgrade." He paused in his admiration of the new vehicle and rubbed the back of his neck. "Is it crazy I miss the old RV... made me kind of feel like we were Scooby and the gang? I was Scooby of course."

This made her genuinely laugh for the first time since last night had gone abysmally bad. Although it looked better than the heap of metal they'd been riding around in, she found herself nostalgic for the older model vehicle as well. "Protector's motor home 2.0 is pretty cool, but I miss the old one too." She gave him a wistful smile that carried more than just a shared appreciation for the previous vehicle. In the smile was the remembered past of just a woman and her faithful dog.

His arms enfolded her in a hug, her face pressed against his shoulder. It reminded her of when she would cuddle with him when he was Max, the dog. She used to rub her cheek against his fur and revel in the fact he was man's best friend: supportive, a good listener, someone who always had her back.

"I know this hasn't been easy, Willow."

Her eyes watered slightly at his words. Partly because of Eli, but mainly because of what Max said. Since they'd left Nashville, she'd been going non-stop: training, learning and moving. There hadn't been a moment to slow down and realize what she left behind. His words made her miss her cramped, but cozy apartment, playing gigs at the Bluebird, grabbing coffee and walking in the park with song lyrics writing themselves in her head as she watched people pass by, she even missed the crummy job a little... okay maybe she didn't actually miss that, but everything else she did. She felt the tears trying to leak out of her eyes and she did her best to suppress them. If she cried now, she might not stop. "Thanks Max. I'll be okay." She sniffled.

As she pulled away from Max, she locked eyes with Eli. Max felt the tension, anger and hostility in her body. She didn't know how she knew this, she just did. Maybe it was because the change in her demeanor raised his hackles even though he wasn't in dog form. A low growl emitted from his throat and his eyes darted around for the threat. His grip on her forearms tightened.

Eli stared at her the way he used to in the office, with that unreadable look where she didn't know what he was thinking.

"It's okay." She tore her gaze away from Eli and looked into Max's face. His expression was taut with a fierce protectiveness. The look conveyed that he would rip someone's head off any minute. "It's okay." She repeated. "I'm okay. There is no danger." She attempted to relax her body so he would calm down.

Gradually the animal instinct that had put him on alert subsided and he released her, but he put his body in front of her like he still expected an attack. Looking back over his shoulder, he questioned her. "What happened? Why did you react like that, anyway? None of the neighbors are out." His head whipped around and looked for the source of her vexation. "We're the only ones out here: me, you, Zoriana, Phaedra and..." He halted. Fear coursed through her body at the thought of him knowing that Eli had rejected her. He turned to her with the unsaid question written all over his face.

She plastered on a fake smile, but her eyes pleaded with him to drop it. "I'm going to put my things on the RV and stake a claim on a seat before everyone else gets on board." The words tumbled out in a rush while she picked up her bag and backed away from him, motioning towards the RV door. "I'll see you inside." She nearly ran flush into the door when she finally turned around.

Inside she found Mathilda playing a game of solitaire at the table. She dropped into the booth opposite her. The young girl didn't look up or acknowledge her. "I was rude to you earlier and I'm sorry." No sense in dragging out the apology. There was no response. "That had nothing to do with you." When Mathilda kept placing the cards in neat piles on the table, she placed her hand over hers to stop her from continuing. "Can you please talk to me? I said I was sorry." It took a moment before Mathilda's eyes raised to meet hers. Her face gave nothing away. After a minute, a little girl grin came out of hiding. "I just wanted to watch you squirm a bit longer." They both giggled.

"You are evil." Willow threw a card at her as she continued to chuckle. In the back of her mind she couldn't help but think about how easily she had forgiven her. Zoriana was still trying to get her to make amends. She was on the verge of asking her about it, but Mathilda spoke.

"What did Cora want?" She fixed the haphazard cards in her game.

"Nothing." Willow stretched back against the seat and looked out the window. Her thoughts went to the letters that sat like a dirty secret in her bag. "I'm gonna put my bag away." She excused herself and went to the bedroom.

After shutting the door, she sagged against it. She hated telling the small white lie, but she wanted to keep the letters to herself for a while longer. Dumping the bag on the bed, she plopped down next to it. Now that she was alone, all the feelings from last night came crashing over her like a huge tidal wave once more. It had been ages since she'd wished for her mother, but right now that's all she wanted was to tell her mother about her bleeding heart and have her console her. She hugged her arms around her torso and gave herself over to the silent sobbing that shook her body. When you were already alone in the world, sometimes rejection had a way of breaking you.

CHAPTER 24

Eli

THINGS HAD GROWN infinitely better between them during the weeks spent at the coven and in one night he'd ruined everything. If her look had been a loaded gun, he'd be dead right now. He'd barely slept last night, wondering and worried if she was okay. Knowing he caused her heartbreak made him feel like the biggest ass. If not for the oath he'd sworn as a Protector he could be with her. How could he make her understand?

Absently, he loaded items into the storage bin on the side of the RV.

"Are you in la la land? I must have called you a thousand times." Phaedra poked him. "What are you so deep in thought about? Or should I say whom."

"Don't. Not today." In his irritation he got a little rough with the packages he'd been stowing.

"Okay, okay. Just stop handling anything before you break it." She took the parcel out of his hand.

He hated being irritable with Phaedra. He knew she meant well, but he was angry with himself, frustrated with the situation and annoyed at his conflicted feelings of honor and duty versus what lay in his heart. "I'm sorry."

"Well, sorry isn't gonna cut it. I need you to get your act together before we get on the road. I'm not riding all over creation with this." She waved her splayed hand up and down his body. "Whatever you need to work out, figure it out and get your ass on the RV. Right now we don't have time for you to be in your feelings." The hard dose of fuck your feelings she doled out may not be what he wanted to hear, but it's what he needed to hear. They had a job to do. She turned on her heel and walked away, leaving him to think about what she'd just said.

Just like he'd done after dealing with another fight with his father, he stuffed his feelings and frustration over the situation with Willow into a small box and tucked it away in the attic of his mind to be dealt with at a later time.

When he climbed on board and looked towards the bedroom, the door was closed. It was for the best. If she holed up in there, the rest of the day he wouldn't have to be constantly reminded of what he was doing his best to not deal with.

Phaedra sat in the driver's seat. "You good?"

"I'm good." He sat in the passenger seat and put on his seat belt. The monstrous vehicle roared to life and Phaedra backed it out of the driveway.

"Where we headed?" Her question held no judgment.

He had no idea. They weren't ready to take the fight to Killian; he just knew they couldn't stay at the coven. They risked putting other lives in jeopardy if he locked in on their location again. They just had to keep moving. "Just drive."

For hours he enjoyed the silence he knew he could count on from Phaedra. He always appreciated that she knew when he needed to be left alone. In that time, Willow stayed ensconced in the bedroom. Zoriana tried to rouse her from her status of hermit crab, but she politely declined. On occasion her singing and the carefully plucked chords of the guitar carried through the door and reached his ears. In an instant, he shoved the sounds out of his mind. It would be too easy for the music and her voice to worm their way inside and cause him to break. He wasn't sure who he was without being a Protector. He'd trained his whole life for this and the thought of tossing it away... scared him. He had to do his duty, which was to teach her and protect her.

He rifled through his bag and found his ear buds. Heavy bass and guitar riffs filled his eardrums as the heavy metal song reached the chorus after he jammed the jack into his phone. He counted on the loud, powerful screams of the lead singer to numb his mind to her heavenly voice.

Once nightfall descended he had Phaedra pull off the road to find a spot for them to make camp. After they set a protection spell around the perimeter they unpacked. The upgrades to the motor home allowed for more people to sleep onboard. Zoriana probably would have shared the king-sized bed that the dining table and chairs turned into with Mathilda if they weren't still at odds with each other. Instead, she rolled out a sleeping bag next to Eli. Phaedra and Max pitched a tent across the meadow for further privacy and Willow, Morgana and Mathilda slept onboard the new RV.

After an awkward dinner that consisted of Phaedra, Max and Morgana trying to keep the conversation going everyone went their separate ways. Willow hadn't once looked in his direction during the meal. She'd dragged her fork around the plate like a sullen teenager and then went straight back to the RV the minute she could. There was a part of him that expected her to blow up and make a scene, yell at him in front of everyone and call him a bastard for what he did. He might have preferred it to the silent treatment she was giving him. He missed being able to talk to her.

His thoughts were interrupted by Zoriana returning from wherever she had been. Once she took a seat on her sleeping bag, her stony gaze stayed locked on the fire. For a short while he allowed her to get lost in whatever thoughts she was engrossed in. If he had one guess, he was sure it had something to do with the daughter that still wasn't speaking to her. "I need you to do something for me tomorrow." Her eyes remained focused on the flames. Lightly, he touched her shoulder. She blinked a few times and then looked at him.

"What?"

"I need you to do something for me tomorrow." His eyes scanned her face. He was growing more concerned over the situation. When he approached his uncle about the two, he didn't seem worried. He'd said something about "women stuff" and said they would work it out soon, but he wasn't convinced.

"Sure." Her eyes lit up at having some job or function that would keep her from her thoughts and he felt less guilty about asking her.

"Would you train Willow tomorrow?" He hadn't expected to see the surprised look that crossed her face.

"But you usually train her?" Her eyebrows knitted together.

"Yes, and now I think she would benefit from a different teacher." It was hard not to sound prickly. Couldn't she just accept the job with no need to question him to death?

"What did you do?"

Apparently, his explanation wasn't good enough. He fell against the log and tipped his head back. "Why do I have to have done anything wrong?"

"You've largely been responsible for Willow's training and now suddenly you just want to relinquish that to someone else?" She folded her arms across her chest. "I'm not buying. Spill. What's going on?"

He huffed. "Fine." Sitting back up, he turned his body to face Zoriana. "After the dinner party my mother gave the night before we left..." Annoyed, he looked away briefly from Zoriana's smug face.

After he tamped down some of his anger, he returned his glare to her face. The Cheshire Cat grin she wore let him know she was unfazed by his irritation. He was an only child, but ever since becoming a Protector he felt like he had sisters with the way Phaedra, Zoriana and Morgana treated him. "When I walked Willow back to her room that night... she told me she had feelings for me and kissed me." His eyes became hooded and his gaze darted around to avoid whatever look she might give him. "I... I rejected her and now she's angry." He hurried to finish so they could stop talking about this.

"Why?" Her tone was laced with so much incredulity; it was hard not to look at her like she'd lost her mind.

"You know why." He seethed through gritted teeth. He

realized his response might make it sound like he cared for Willow. Straightening his posture he dropped his anger and tried to look unaffected. "I think you're under the assumption I return her feelings. You would be wrong." He hoped his matter-of-fact tone would squash whatever she was thinking.

"But you do." She returned his tone.

His head whipped around to stare directly at her. "No, I don't. You don't know what you're talking about."

"Just admit that you like her."

He sighed in exasperation and his shoulders slumped in defeat. "Even if I admitted you were right, what does it matter? You and I both know the commandment says it's forbidden for me to..." The look he gave Zoriana was full of torture. He squeezed his eyes shut in frustration before he exhaled. The next words were a soft plea. "Can we just drop this, please? Will you train her or not?"

She regarded him quietly for several breaths. "Yes."

"Thank you." It was still early, but he turned over on his side away from her.

Phaedra kept warning him away from his feelings and reminding him of his duty and here Zoriana was acting like he was a man that had a choice. He was already wrestling with his own conflicting emotions, the last thing he needed was to add everyone else's opinion to the mix.

Please let sleep come quickly.

The sounds of Zoriana getting comfortable in her sleeping bag mingled with the crackling of the fire as the dying embers turned to ash. As he lay there trying to go to sleep, there was a part of him that wanted to communicate with her telepathically, given it was probably the only way she would listen to him but he wouldn't invade her mind or take away her choice. If she ever spoke to him again, it would be on her terms. He missed being peppered with a million questions and listening to her talk. After being thrown together for over two months it was weird not talking to her. The last twenty-four hours without her speaking to him had felt like someone put out the sun.

Damn. I have it bad.

To make matters worse, in the distance he was sure he heard the faint sounds of Phaedra and Max's lovemaking. Maybe they were attempting to be quiet, but it wasn't working. He grabbed his ear buds from his pocket and stuffed them into his ears before he plugged the jack into his phone and turned the volume up. There was no way he would listen to them all night.

When was the last time he'd gotten laid?

Go to sleep. He told himself. There was no sense in thinking about that when that train of thought would only lead to someone he was trying not to think about.

***

The next day he woke up early and left the camp before anyone else was awake. Hours later, while he scavenged the woods for plants that might be useful he hoped that Willow remembered what he told her about always carrying the dagger with her. Now that they were back out on the road, it was imperative she have the blade on her at all times. When he gave it to her, he hadn't told her he'd imbued it with different magical spells, one of which was a locator spell. If she were ever abducted, they could track her and find her.

Even though she had her fae powers, they were new to her, and she was still learning how to use them. They still hadn't figured out all of her abilities and everything she was capable of. The dagger was a practical weapon she could use if she needed to.

He dragged his thoughts back to his problem with Willow. Avoidance wasn't the answer, but he thought it was best for now. He didn't want her to think he abandoned her training because of what happened between them. They were both adults. He would just have to talk to her and see if they could put aside any differences and focus on her training. Willow was a reasonable woman. Right?

He pondered the thought all the way back to the camp. When he arrived, he found Max and Phaedra cozy by the fire. Max whispered in her ear and nipped her neck in a playful manner. Eli quickly averted his gaze from the romantic scene. When he heard her soft, teasing giggle he cleared his throat loudly. Phaedra wasn't the type of woman that giggled so he felt like he'd intruded on something private.

By the time he joined them at the fire the two had separated. Max showed no signs of being awkward or uncomfortable and from what he'd learned about him he was not a man that was easily embarrassed. On the other hand, he knew his best friend liked her privacy. He wouldn't be making any jokes about them being booed up unless he wanted to sport a black eye. "Where's everyone?" He poured himself some coffee.

"Zoriana's training Willow. Mathilda and Morgana are inside..." She gestured towards the RV. "They're working on some potions."

He looked towards the direction he believed Zoriana and Willow would have gone for her training and reminded himself he vowed to set things right between them, as right as he could make them. Part of him wanted to charge off into the meadow and search for them so he could deal with everything now. Willow must be rubbing off on him, because he'd never been an impatient man. When it came to her, he did things he wouldn't have done before.

Phaedra's eyes were burning a hole into his back. He'd been staring in that direction for too long. The last thing he wanted was another lecture. He sat on the ground and sipped at his coffee. Hopefully, the wait wouldn't be so bad.

Nearly three cups of coffee and an hour later, he caught sight of them. He got up and headed towards them. The plan was to get her alone away from the camp so they could talk without prying eyes or ears eavesdropping on what they said. Willow was animatedly talking to Zoriana about something, but the minute she saw him approaching she stopped. The two women waited for him to come to them. His eyes didn't leave Willow's face despite the death glare she was giving him. "Zoriana, could I have a minute alone with Willow?"

Zoriana gave her a look to make sure she didn't mind being left alone with him. When she gave her a nod of confirmation, his aunt left. Once she was several feet away he spoke. "I was hoping we could tal..."

She cut him off. "What do you want?" The sweet lips he'd had the pleasure of kissing were twisted into a frown, while her eyes scowled at him. Her hands were wrapped around her body, much like they were the other night.

Better to just go straight for the most hurtful lie he could think of. "I'm sorry about the other night. I shouldn't have led you on like that. I don't feel that way about you... I don't feel the same way about you that you feel about me."

It was like watching a row of dominoes fall, the way her face fell. Whatever she'd been expecting him to say, it hadn't been that. The angry look she sported seconds ago must have been false bravado. "But... but you kissed me back." It was impossible not to miss the way her lip quivered and her eyes became glassy with unshed tears.

"Yes, I did, but it was because I felt gratitude for what you said to my father at dinner and... you looked beautiful that night. It was hard to resist you, but that's exactly why I stopped it."

"You don't have to patronize me." Her gaze shifted away from him and she took a stuttering breath.

He hated hurting her like this, but he continued. "I'm here to protect you. It's my job to keep you safe, not be your boyfriend. This talk was to see if we... if you could put your feelings aside and have us resume our training."

The look she gave him could have leveled a building with no explosives. His eyes stayed locked on her watery gaze. It was excruciating watching her internal struggle as she did her best to compose her features and not give way to whatever emotions she was feeling. She dropped her hands to her sides. "You've said what you came to say. You're my bodyguard and my teacher, nothing more." The disdain that contorted her beautiful face before she stalked off made him feel like the biggest asshole. He turned and watched her walk away. Her shoulders were squared and her head was held high like she was telling the world that his rejection of her wouldn't break her. He hoped it didn't.

After his conversation with Willow, he convinced Phaedra to spar with him out in the meadow. Stripped to the waist and covered in a fine sheen of perspiration he swung the staff around hoping to catch Phaedra off guard. No such luck. She blocked his move and quickly countered with one of her own that had him ducking to avoid a swing that would have connected and knocked the wind out of him.

"We've been at this for over an hour and your head is not here." She confirmed her revelation by swinging her staff around her head in a wide arc before bringing it back down in a swift motion that caught him on his thigh. He knew she'd held back because the stinging pain in his leg was a lot less than what it usually felt like when he got hit by her.

"Okay, you're right. I'm distracted. Let's call it a day." With his staff held in one hand he bent to retrieve his shirt.

"Do you want to talk about it?" Phaedra leaned on her staff with both hands and eyed him.

He was about to tell her he was good and she didn't need to be concerned when a yell was followed by what sounded like a small explosion. Both of them gave each other a sharp look before they broke into a run headed back towards camp. Once they rounded the edge of the forest that blocked their view from the clearing where the camp was located, the sight of a swarm of attacking vampires greeted them. They quickly joined the fight.

He hurled a fireball at the nearest vampire, his eyes steadily scanning the melee for Willow. Was she safe? Had they taken her? Then his eyes landed on Zoriana fighting with a statuesque, Middle Eastern women, with expertly delivered and timed fighting skills. Unlike the other vampires nearby that weren't doing a good job at evading magic, she could block and avoid the spells Zoriana directed at her. She noticed him too and their eyes locked in a challenge. If Killian had sent someone like her and not only expendables, then they meant to take her. He quickly dispatched with the vampire he'd been fighting with and made his way towards her.

CHAPTER 25

Willow

IN A SPLIT second she went from thinking about Eli's stinging delivery that he didn't return her feelings to focusing on staying alive. The vampires seemed to come out of nowhere and then they were everywhere. She wasn't sure how many of them there were. She couldn't see through the fog that had cropped up. Where had it come from? It must have been something that arrived with the presence of the vampires because it had been a bright clear day and now it was shrouded in mist.

'WILLOW? WHERE ARE YOU?' Eli's voice sounded inside her head.

Despite their earlier conversation, she'd never been so happy to hear his voice. 'ELI.' She searched for him, but it was hard to see through the fog and bodies that ran and fought all around her.

Phaedra was locked in combat with two vampires. One of them went flying backwards when she blasted her with what looked like a bolt of electricity. The other vampire advanced on Phaedra only to get bashed in the head with the blunt end of her staff. She was a force to be reckoned with. Nearby, Max had shifted into his werewolf form. Four different vampires were doing their best to take him down. Before she turned away, she saw one's head go flying after Max's large claws swiped it clean off its shoulders.

'WILLOW GET TO THE RV AND HIDE BENEATH IT.'

She knew he'd given her orders to stay out of the fight, but she couldn't sit by while everyone fought on her behalf. It wasn't exactly like she was helpless. She had powers. He was trying to do his job and protect her, but she couldn't listen to what he said. She had to fight.

Ignoring what he'd said, she saw Mathilda being swarmed while trying to fend them off. No one must have been close to the RV when the battle broke out. Not that anyone needed the weapons they'd purchased from Samson, but she couldn't help thinking the vervain gun might come in handy right about now.

She ran towards the group attacking Mathilda and raised her hand, palm facing outward, focused and shot a beam of energy at one of the vampires. It was hard not to be a little pleased with herself after having practiced in mock fights how to use her powers and to see it working during the real thing. She hated that her brain was having that inappropriate thought at this moment when lives hung in the balance.

Mentally, she shook the thought away and aimed an energy blast at another bloodsucker. With her help, Mathilda emerged from the corner they had backed her into. She raised her hand and some invisible force picked up a vampire and threw them across the field.

Again her eyes searched for Eli. She knew he'd be furious with her for not staying out of this. They'd probably argue about it, but she would make him understand that she wasn't some damsel in distress that needed other people to do her fighting for her.

A vampire charged her, knocking them both to the ground. The breath flew out of her lungs after they hit. She reacted quickly and shot a stream of energy at him while she scrambled to her feet. Adrenaline coursed through her veins. She took off running, in case the vampire gave chase. Not that she could really outrun the vampire. There was no outrunning their super speed. She'd seen enough movies to know, but it didn't stop her from trying.

Seconds later she was shoved to the ground from behind. When she attempted to get up, someone pulled her leg out from under her and flipped her over like she weighed nothing, like she was a rag doll. She struck the ground again with more force. Air was pushed out of her lungs and her head smacked the ground hard. She was dazed and tried to shake herself out of the stupor. It wasn't quick enough because suddenly she was lifted from the ground and held aloft in the air.

She was unprepared for the amount of strength the vampire was capable of. With one hand the vampire gripped her throat and lifted her until her feet dangled. The cold hand wrapped around her throat was gradually cutting off her air supply. She flailed and kicked, while she tried desperately to remove the hand from her neck. The vampire's smile of pure satisfaction reminded her of Killian's.

The edges of her eyesight were going black. She had to do something soon or she would lose consciousness. Her frenzied mind remembered she had the dagger in her waistband. As she continued to struggle to release herself with one hand, her other hand trembled with exertion at reaching for the blade. Her fingers were almost there. Just a little more. She felt a small measure of relief when her finger latched onto the hilt. Spasms and twitching kept her from pulling the dagger right away, while her feet continued to scramble, toeing the air for solid ground.

Her eyes bulged and watered with the effort to breathe; any second she would lose the fight and go to sleep just like the vampire wanted. That thought revived her with new energy. Her hand clutched the dagger and yanked it from her waistband. She wasted no time in plunging it directly into the vampire's chest. She had no idea if vampires still had hearts that could bleed or stop beating, but the move was enough to catch her off guard and give Willow the upper hand. Once the bloodsucker looked down to see what punctured her chest, Willow lifted her hand and blasted her in the face with a burst of energy. The vampire released her.

Instantly breath returned to her lungs as the force of the blast launched the vampire off her feet and sent her spiraling into the trunk of a nearby tree. Coughs wracked Willow's body when she fell to the ground and rolled onto her side. Battle still waged around her, but the only thing she could concern herself with was sucking in air. Her throat was raw and breathing burned with every wheeze she took. She rose to her hands and knees as she sputtered and choked.

Screams and sounds of earth being raised or blown apart and spells being cast surrounded her on all sides. Her vision was still spotty as she shakily pushed herself to her feet.

"WILLOW!"

The sound of someone screaming her name ripped through the air over all the other noises. When she looked towards the direction of the voice, she stared across the distance into Eli's terrified eyes. His whole body was paralyzed with fear. Then she noticed the Middle Eastern woman that had been in one of her Killian dreams standing a few feet behind him. Her eyes shifted back to Eli.

Why does he look so scared? She was all right. The side of her mouth tilted into a lopsided, goofy grin that comes with being punch-drunk or in shock. She raised a hand to wave to him. It wasn't normal to be grinning when all around you war was being waged. She knew that, yet she couldn't help the reaction she was having.

Something pierced her side and caused a pain unlike any she'd ever felt before. Tears seeped from her eyes. She looked down to find a spear sticking through her side. Disbelief was the only emotion that clouded her already foggy brain at that moment.

There's a spear in my side.

Her shaky hand grabbed a hold of the wood that was now slick and coated with her blood. She pulled her hand away and looked at the smear of crimson red that colored her palm and fingers.

I guess I'm not invulnerable.

One of the spiritual faery abilities she didn't possess would have come in handy right about now.

'WILLOW, COME WITH ME AND HE CAN HEAL YOU. HE CAN MAKE ALL YOUR PAIN GO AWAY. YOU NEVER HAVE TO HURT AGAIN.'

It wasn't Eli's voice she heard in her head. When she looked up and looked into the woman's eyes, she knew it was her voice that was attempting to coax her to give herself over to Killian willingly. Could she read her thoughts and discern how much agony she was in? She shook away the voice that was trying to seduce her to give up and let Killian win. A spasm of pain surged through her body and made her gasp.

When her eyes found Eli again, she gave him one last smile before she slumped to the ground in a faint.

CHAPTER 26

Eli

WHEN HE LOOKED up from the reprieve in his battle with the female vampire that appeared to be the leader, another vampire threw a spear at Willow. In that moment, he felt powerless. The female vampire roared behind him when the spear hit its mark. An instant later, the vampire who threw the weapon dropped dead. He didn't have time to question how she'd been able to do that, he just knew he had to get to Willow.

Killian needed Willow alive so why would that vampire mortally wound her? Unless it was a mistake. Errors happened often in the heat of battle. Her back was to him, so he hadn't seen who he was aiming at, he just knew it was the enemy. Mistake or not it pissed this woman off and made that vampire's life forfeit.

All he could think about was getting to her, but before he could do that, he had to dispense with these monsters. "Gladius." He stated and watched the staff in his hands change into a sword. In a quick motion, he spun around and swung the blade toward the woman's throat. Anyone else would have been decapitated, but she had expected his move and burst into a swarm of bats before the blade connected.

The retreating swarm must have been a signal to the other vampires because they either ran away using their super speed or vanished into the mist and fog, which receded and disappeared once they all fled.

With the battle over and the impending threat departed, he charged across the meadow like a steaming locomotive gone off its rails.

Once he reached her, he dropped next to her limp, seemingly lifeless body. When he recalled the way she looked at him after realizing she'd been wounded, something twisted in his gut. Thankfully, she'd landed on her side and hadn't caused any further damage with her fall. He placed his hand on her stomach. "Sana." A faint white light glowed beneath his hands as he tried to summon enough magic to heal her, but barely anything happened.

Dirt and debris kicked up as Phaedra skidded to his side. "How bad is she?"

His eyes darted around to the various parts of Willow's injured body. The cut on her forehead, the purplish choke marks that lined her throat then his eyes finally took in the horror of the spear that impaled her. Blood oozed from the wound that could prove fatal. Something took hold of his tongue and wouldn't let him speak. He was in shock. Fear wound itself tightly around him like an anaconda readying him for a snack.

"How bad?" After several seconds of his lips moving and no words coming out Phaedra shoved him out of the way and started to tend to Willow. He landed on his ass in the dirt and watched in terror.

"Sana." Phaedra tried to heal her with her magic, but it was the same effect. Nothing.

Mathilda, Zoriana, Morgana and Max all crowded around, trying to help save Willow's life. They talked around him, but he couldn't have told you what was spoken. The last words he'd said to her played on a loop inside his head. He'd fed her a bunch of lies and hid behind his duty, instead of telling her how he felt. Now he may never get to tell her. If she died, she'd never know. All she would have would be his righteous honor he'd shoved down her throat.

Max was already off and moving when Phaedra's voice penetrated his thoughts. "Her being half faery is what's keeping her alive right now. I need you to pull your head from your ass and get it together. We're all too weak to use magic to save her after expending a ton of magic during that battle. We have to do this the old-fashioned way." She snapped off the back end of the spear. "Whatever you have to say to her you can say once we save her life, but right now we need you." She never spared a glance in his direction the whole time she chastised him for losing his shit. "Go strip the bed of sheets and bring them back here. I already have Max boiling water." She placed her hand on the spear that still protruded from Willow's side. "Morgana go find the healing salve I made of yarrow, self heal, comfrey and rose. Mathilda make sure nothing will be in our way when we carry her into the RV. Zoriana you'll stay here with me."

For a minute, they were all stuck in place. Everyone concerned for Willow and on edge over the lack of being able to use their magic to heal her.

"Move!" The sharp crack of Phaedra's order sent them scattering in all directions to do her bidding. He was glad to have something to do, to keep his mind occupied.

After finding whatever clean sheets he could he physically tore them to strips while using his magic to tear more. At least it allowed him to do that. When he returned, the rest of the spear lay to the side and they had torn away most of her shirt. More blood was pooled beneath her. Zoriana had her hand pressed into the wound. The blood loss made her beautiful brown skin look nearly as white as the sheets he carried. She still had not regained consciousness and for that he was thankful because she would have been in agonizing pain.

"Give those to me." When Phaedra barked the order at him he moved closer and handed over the sheets.

Morgana ran up with the salve. "I found it." She was out of breath.

Max hurried over with the cauldron of boiling water. The iron pot landed with a heavy thud on the ground. Phaedra dipped in some of the sheet. "Did you bring the other thing?" Everyone looked to Max to see what she referred to. He held up the steel tent peg that now glowed an orange-red at one end.

"What are you going to do with that?" In the state he was in, he asked stupid questions he already knew the answer to.

"We have to cauterize the wound." Her voice was forceful before her eyes swept over Willow's flushed face. When she turned her eyes back to him, her features softened and her voice was gentler as she gave him yet another explanation why things had to be done this way. "Her wound could be a fatal one and right now our magic isn't strong enough to heal her. In the morning, after our magic has had time to replenish, we should be able to heal it, but right now we have to stop this bleeding. This is the only way." Phaedra looked at him with something akin to pity and sympathy. "I need you to hold her down. She's likely to wake up when that touches her skin."

His jaw tightened, but he moved to the top of her head and placed his knees firmly in the dirt before placing his hands on her shoulders. Phaedra finished wiping as much blood away as she could so they could have a clear view to the wound. "Now." Once she gave the word, Max pressed the scorching end of the peg to Willow's skin. The only sound that could be heard was the sizzling of her flesh before she came to.

She howled and shrieked. On either side of her Zoriana and Mathilda held onto her arms and hands. Her head tilted back, and she stared into his eyes. The wild, tortured look on her face branding itself forever into his brain, much like the red-hot poker was doing to her flesh. Max took the rod away so they could turn her onto her side and he pressed the metal to the back of the wound. Her cries pierced his heart. Seconds later, she passed out again.

When he finished Morgana and Phaedra worked quickly to pack either side of the wound with salve before they began to wrap her midsection with the dried strips he'd brought back. Once they had her bandaged, they put her on a blanket and carried her into the bedroom aboard the RV.

"I'll start out sitting with her... unless..." Mathilda looked to him.

Now that she was stable he wanted to sit with her, but all he could feel was guilt over not getting to her fast enough or using his magic. He was supposed to protect her. Even though logic and reason told him that either way he wouldn't have been fast or quick enough he couldn't stop binging on guilt cookies. "No... you sit with her." He left the RV. Phaedra followed him.

"We can't stay here."

"I know. I'll drive." He'd already shoved items into the storage area at the bottom of the RV. As he collected their things, his eyes kept being drawn to the blood-stained grass where her blood began to congeal. The setting sun caught the reflection of something shiny in the grass. He walked over to see what it was and found her dagger. He turned it over in his hands a few times and then wiped the blade off on his pants. When she recovered, he'd return it to her.

No one said anything to him. Everyone else except for Mathilda worked quickly to gather everything up so they could get on the road. Max made quick work of burning any dead vampire bodies left behind. Zoriana cast a spell to change the outside appearance of the mobile home. Thankfully, they could use simple magic such as that. Healing required so much of them, especially with a wound like Willow's. It angered him there was nothing they could do for her until later. He just hoped it wouldn't be too late.

Within thirty minutes they were pulling out of the clearing and onto the dirt road that led back out to the main road. Unlike the times before where they traveled with the sounds of talking, laughter, music playing or a card game filling the space, there was complete silence.

Eli had put his torn shirt over his grime-covered body before he took his seat behind the wheel. Everyone still wore battle stained clothes. The metallic smell of blood hung in the air, but no one said anything. It wasn't just the blood of the fallen vampires that left an odor. The stench reminded them that Willow lay wounded, unconscious and clinging to life in the bedroom, because they failed to protect her. He failed to protect her.

After hours of aimless driving, Phaedra touched his shoulder. "Instead of camping, we need to find a motel." She must have seen that he meant to keep driving if it meant driving to the ends of the earth to keep Willow safe. "She needs to rest if she's going to get better and the constant jostling from this vehicle will not help her." She knew what to say to appeal to his logic and reason. Once she used Willow, he would comply.

He pulled onto the next off-ramp and they found a fleabag motel. Zoriana used magic to make the RV invisible once they parked it at the back of the parking lot. After they paid for the rooms, Morgana and Mathilda went inside to once again use magic to sanitize and sterilize the room that Willow would occupy, then they carried her in and lay her on the bed.

Blood stained her cheek and mud matted her hair. She looked feverish. Fear knotted his gut and twisted around it like barbed wire.

What if she gets worse? What if she doesn't survive the night?

"I'll clean and redress her wound tonight. In the morning we'll be recovered enough to heal her and then give her a bath." Phaedra spoke to everyone, but he was sure she was saying those things to ease his mind.

"I'll stay with her tonight." Max spoke up.

"Get some sleep." This time Phaedra spoke directly to him. "There is nothing more you can do for her right now."

He left the room with Mathilda, Morgana and Zoriana who each tried to console and comfort him, but he shook them off and headed to his motel room. His restless mind was too wound up for sleep. Once he pulled the curtains and shut off the lights, he dragged a chair towards the window to wait for Phaedra to pass. He knew her room was further down and she had to walk past his to get there. Once she was inside, he would go to her. Twenty minutes later, Phaedra walked by his room, but not without stopping at the door. The complete silence and darkness must have stopped her from knocking. Even if she had knocked, he would have pretended to be asleep and not answered.

The click of her room door let him know when she went inside. Like a soldier biding his time before his mission began, he waited and waited and waited some more before he finally slipped from his room; secure in the thought everyone had gone to bed and wouldn't hear him. When he exited, he turned the knob to make sure the door wouldn't squeak and give him away. He walked back down to Willow's room and placed his hand on the locked door. "Recludo." The door swung open slightly.

When he stepped inside, he saw Max sleeping in dog form at the end of her bed. He looked over at him. Eli was afraid he'd bark and put his pointer finger against his lips in a request for silence. Max's head dropped and he whined.

He sat on the side of the bed and gazed at her. Even though the room was only bathed in the moonlight that streamed from the windows he could see her skin was flushed. When he placed the backs of his fingers against her cheek, she burned like she had a furnace living inside of her. She appeared to be having a fever dream. Her eyes moved restlessly beneath her eyelids and her body twitched and spasmed from whatever craziness her mind conjured up in its delirium. It pained him to think of her dreaming with no escape from whatever hellish world her mind imagined that could include Killian. He had to make her better.

"I'm sorry I didn't protect you." He whispered to her.

Moving his body closer, he placed his hands over the newly bandaged wound and shut his eyes. "Sana." A faint white light glowed beneath his hands, but instantly he felt an intense pressure in his skull. His nose bled, ruining the white sheets that covered her. It was too much, but he had to try. He tried to push the limits of his powers past what he was physically capable of in his sleep deprived, weakened physical and mental state. The pain in his head increased.

"I knew you wouldn't listen." When Phaedra had entered the room, he didn't know. "Addormio."

The next thing he saw was only blackness.

***

If you plan to continue with this series, there's an epilogue...but I suggest you stop here if you don't like cliffhangers and don't plan to continue. Thanks for reading!

CHAPTER 27

Willow

WHILE HER BODY fought off the infection that happened after being wounded she'd fallen in and out of restless, frenzied nightmarish dreams. Flashes and snippets of noise and sound permeated her unconscious mind, but she couldn't make sense of anything. It reminded her of scenes ripped out of the film *Jacob's Ladder*. Unfortunately, she couldn't wake herself. For a moment she wondered if she was dead, then she heard Eli's voice talking to her. Maybe she imagined it.

Morgana and Zoriana had been by her bedside when she opened her eyes. They mentioned they healed her, but she would have a scar. She'd been groggy and fatigued down to her bones.

For the first few days after she woke up, despite only having the scar where the spear had ripped through muscle and flesh, her body was severely weak.

Phaedra had been the ringleader in confining her to bed so she would heal and recover quickly. They each took turns sitting with her and sleeping in her room each night. One day in her recovery saw her battling an intense migraine, but thankfully by the next day it was gone.

It was now six days since she awakened and she hadn't seen him once. Where was Eli? Why hadn't he come to see her? Even though their last conversation had left her hurt and angry, it didn't mean she didn't want to see him. When she asked about him, no one would answer her questions. She'd seen him right before she passed out from her wound. He hadn't been killed had he? If he was dead, why didn't they just tell her instead of drawing out her worry? A part of her was tempted to force her way from the room and go in search of him.

Now she was growing angry he hadn't come to see her. If he were alive why hadn't he visited to at least tell her he was glad she recovered? Did he care so little for her? It pricked her heart and her pride he possibly roamed around outside the four walls she occupied for nearly a week and he hadn't set foot inside once.

When she wasn't spending every waking minute thinking about him, she enjoyed Max's company and the nights he slept next to her in his dog form like he used to. It was a huge comfort to her to reach out and feel his smooth black fur beneath her palm.

On the night of that sixth day, she lay in bed waiting for whoever was staying with her. She was feeling ninety percent stronger and healthier and was sure she could get out of bed, but Phaedra insisted she wait one more day so she appeased her.

She leaned against the headboard flipping channels when the door opened. "Well, it's about time. I was getting restless." Her voice tapered off when she lifted her eyes and found Eli standing in the doorway.

He's alive.

She'd never seen him look the way he did. The only word she could use to describe his appearance was scruffy. If she was honest she kind of liked it. He'd been clean-shaven before, but now he sported a heavy five o'clock shadow. Gone were the button-down shirts and slacks. He wore jeans and a t-shirt and still made it look sexy. She became fully aware at the moment she only wore a tank top, bra and panties. The thin sheet that draped over her lower half was the only thing that covered her near nakedness.

For a while, neither of them said a word. They just stared at each other. She finally broke the silence. "Why haven't you come before now? I... I was thinking you died, and they just didn't know how to tell me." She looked him up and down once more and she became incensed over his callousness. He knew the way she felt, but let her lay here day after day thinking something had happened to him. "Now that I see you're alive and well you can leave." Her eyes flicked back to the TV, and she resumed channel surfing.

Instead of leaving like she expected, he stepped inside and closed the door. She let out an exasperated huff. Why was he still here? Even when he sat on the edge of the bed, she continued to ignore him. Several minutes passed, and he said nothing, just watched her. She couldn't take anymore. "Why are you here? What do you want?" The words came out through clenched teeth. The anger coursing through her body was like a tightly coiled spring. She was ready to explode at him.

Still, he only stared and for a moment it reminded her of the Eli she knew at work, the one that had only been her disdainful co-worker; not the witch, the teacher, the protector and friend she cared for deeply. She couldn't stop the angry tears forming in her eyes that threatened to undo her carefully contained volatile emotions. "What do you want?" The raw torture and pain she felt were on display and no longer concealed. The question was asking more than just what he wanted this minute or why he was here.

For the space of a heartbeat they stared into each other's eyes and then the impassive expression he wore transformed to something beatific. "I want you."

They reached for each other at the same time. With the press of his warm lips against hers, her anger melted away, replaced by a blissfulness that made her replete and settled into her bones. They were both on their knees in the middle of the bed, kissing with abandon. His tongue was exploring every crevice, every nook and cranny of her mouth like it might unearth some secret he didn't know about her. It made her body ache. For a second he leaned away from her. "I'm not hurting you am I?"

"No." Impatient to be in his arms again, she pulled him back to her and sucked his bottom lip into her mouth before she bit it. He grunted.

There was a minor, dull ache that persisted in her side, but nothing would stop this from happening right now.

His hands palmed her ass and then slide down her legs. In a quick movement he had her on her back. He parted her thighs and knelt between them. One-handed he pulled his shirt over his head and tossed it to the floor.

"Are you trying to impress me?" She looked up at him, her tone playful.

His hands rubbed up and down the front of her thighs. "Is it working?" An impish grin spread across his face.

In answer, she pulled him down for another kiss that left them both breathless. He pushed up onto his knees and pulled her shirt over her head and then made quick work of her bra. She lay beneath him clad in only her panties. He salivated over her ample bosom like a cartoon wolf before he dove in and lavished them with all of his attention. His tongue curled around her nipple and made it form into a stiff peak. The sensation she felt from his rough tongue on her skin made her head roll to the side and a moan fell from her lips. It really sent her over the edge when he sucked her nipple into his mouth and let his fingers toy with the other one. Her thighs gripped him and she tried to rub herself against his body, needing something to quell the slow burn that was quickly turning into a raging inferno. When he went to move away from her so, he could remove her panties she stopped him with two words. "Rip them."

He didn't need to be told twice because in the next second she heard fabric being torn and then her ruined panties were discarded. The kisses he placed all over her body scalded her and had her craving more. He kissed a trail to her belly button, where he nestled between her legs and placed kisses down the inside of her thighs until his mouth reached her weeping core. She'd become wet from the sheer anticipation of his mouth reaching its goal. The hungry look in his eyes when he reached her pussy made her legs quiver. He stared at her unflinching as he prolonged putting his mouth exactly where they both wanted him. It was exquisite torture. When he finally swiped his tongue over the sensitive area her back arched off the bed.

As he drank deeply from her sweet nectar, they were both lost. "You taste so good," He breathed out as he lapped at her. His arms curled around her thighs, holding her in place for an intense ravishing.

Her fingers knotted themselves in his hair and she pushed him deeper. While his tongue licked, sucked and tasted her, he inserted his finger and curled it just enough so he rubbed her G-spot. She nearly came off the bed when he made contact.

'YOU LOVE THAT DON'T YOU?' When he entered her mind all she could do was let out a loud groan to let him know just how much she loved it. The wolfish grin he sported on any other man might have annoyed her, but he truly knew what he was doing. He could grin like that all he wanted as long as he kept making her feel like she was about to melt into a pool of ecstasy.

He nipped and sucked on her clit as his finger penetrated her, driving her into a frenzy of need.

'CUM FOR ME.' He commanded.

The fact that he could say that to her without having to stop his mouth from what he was doing turned her on even more. She pulled at his hair again when she felt the spasm in her belly that told her she was about to have the most glorious orgasm. "I'm gonna cum." She bit down to keep from crying out.

'LET ME HEAR YOU BABE. TELL ME HOW GOOD I'M MAKING YOU FEEL.' He sped up the pace of his tongue and finger and before she knew it she was coming undone. An intense burst of color happened behind her eyes and she was seeing stars while she screamed her release.

'YES BABY! JUST LIKE THAT.' He urged her on. Neither of them seemed to care that they were in a crappy motel that no doubt had paper-thin walls. All she knew was he'd made her explode with one of the best orgasms she'd ever had and she wanted more. Yes, please and thank you.

Right now she wanted to feel the big monster swinging between his legs inside of her. Would she be able to take all of him? "I need you." Her breathy plea reached his ears, and he looked up at her. His hungry look had now turned ravenous. With one final swipe he released her legs and got up from the bed.

She rubbed her breasts and played with her nipples while she watched him from the bed. He removed his jeans slowly and sensually like he was her private dancer, putting on a show. He was torturing her that's what he was doing.

Now that she could see his naked chest she took in his well-defined pecs and washboard abs. When the jeans came off, she really started to drool. The boxer briefs he wore showed off the taut muscles in his thighs. His legs looked powerful, but she knew it was nothing compared to what hid in his boxers. He gave her a wicked grin and then removed his last remaining garment. Once he stood back up, she could see the bulbous, pink head of his long, thick throbbing member that stood at attention ready to please and service her. A pearly drop of pre-cum glistened from the tip and only one thought crossed her mind. *What does he taste like?*

Her eyes were riveted to his swollen cock as he fished the condom from his pants' pocket and put it on. She wanted him back between her legs, now. Her fingers slid between her parted thighs and she rubbed the bundle of nerves that were wet with her arousal while she maintained eye contact with him. That got him moving quickly. In no time he was on the bed.

There was no communication needed. Her thighs fell open in invitation and he crawled towards her like a sleek jungle cat that had just cornered its prey. She wanted him to devour her. He leaned on his elbows over her. The heat that emanated from his body was making her hotter and wetter. 'ARE YOU READY FOR ME?' His dick gently rubbed against her clit in such a delicious way all she could do was nod in answer to his question.

He kissed her chin and reached between them to position the tip of his cock against her entrance. They both watched it disappear inside of her. After that he looked back up at her as he slid the rest of the way inside. "Fuck."

After the slow invasion of her pussy, he was no longer speaking to her through her mind. He buried his head in the crook of her neck while he took a ragged breath. "You're so fucking tight." He gently bit her shoulder.

It took several seconds before he began to move inside of her. Her walls contracted on him tightly and he groaned. Inside, he filled and touched every part of her. The pull and drag of him moving felt so good her eyes rolled back into her head. He came up on his knees while still impaled within her walls. The desire she saw in his eyes made her tremble and ache. He placed his hands at the bend of her knee and pushed, opening her up even wider so he could fill her completely. When he plowed into her with such force, it had her toes curling. As he moved, he removed one hand from her leg and rubbed her glistening clit. The sensation had her purring like a contented cat, and it wasn't long before the purr morphed into a loud moan.

"Baby." She groaned when his dick hit a sweet spot. "Oh, that feels so good."

Both of their bodies were slick with sweat. He leaned over her and thrust deeply, kissing her mouth hard. She welcomed his weight. She wrapped her legs around his waist, wanting him pressed against her when she came.

The sex was amazing. She wanted to prolong her climax, but there was no way she could stop it. She gripped his forearms. The effects of her orgasm shook her body, her thighs trembled, and she moaned and cursed and called his name. "Fuck! Eli!" More expletives fell from her mouth as the last of her tremors subsided. Her walls pulsated around his hard, throbbing cock. He kissed her shoulder and increased his speed. His balls pounded against her ass. She could feel he was close.

"Fuck babe, I'm close." He nipped her neck.

She hooked her arms around him and enjoyed the ride. He was pushing her to a second orgasm. It was rough and wild and she loved every minute. Thrusting deeply several more times, he came with a loud groan of pleasure. She clenched around his throbbing cock when she came a second time, moments after he did, milking every drop of cum from him.

They clung to each other in the afterglow. Sweetly, he kissed her neck and shoulder before he slowly pulled out of her so he could discard the condom. A short while later he rejoined her in the bed. He pulled her towards him and kissed her forehead. On his back, he was sprawled out, with one arm cradling her to his side. They shared a few tender kisses before her head dropped to his chest. A delicious ache was between her legs and she wore a satisfied smile.

For a while they lay together without speaking until she remembered some things that were running through her mind when he'd shown up hours ago. "What changed your mind? I thought you didn't care for me?" Her fingers stroked his chest where her head lay. She looked up at him while she awaited his answer. It seemed silly to be asking this after what they'd just done, but she needed to know.

His jaw flexed while he returned her gaze. His eyes never seemed bluer than they did right now. "I lied. I'm sorry." He looked contrite. "It was the only way I could try to distance myself from you. Push you away. My feelings were just as strong as yours, but my sense of duty clouded my judgment." His fingers smoothed over her curls before he caressed her cheek. She sighed and closed her eyes briefly before she pressed closer, soaking up his touch. "Seeing you hurt right in front of me, made me realize I was a complete idiot. I almost lost you and it scared me." He swallowed back a lump of emotion and cleared his throat, probably replaying those pained, torturous moments of seeing her wounded. "I know the oath I swore, but duty isn't more important than..." His eyes raked over her face with a tenderness she never thought him capable of. "Love."

When she looked into his eyes, she knew he was telling the truth. It was true for her too. She cared just as deeply for him. She loved Eli, but she wasn't letting him off that easy. "Why didn't you come see me when they told you I was awake?"

He sat up against the pillows and pulled her up with him. His big hands cradled her face. "I'm sure you're learning what an idiot I can be." They both chuckled, but then his expression turned serious. "I felt tremendous guilt over you getting fatally injured like that. It shouldn't have happened. Not on my watch."

Willow couldn't suppress the giggle that escaped and then it turned into a full belly laugh the more she tried to suppress it. His hands fell away from her face. Through her laughing, she saw his face contorted in confusion and then it shifted to mild anger. "I'm not so sure what's so funny. I'm pouring out my heart here and you're laughing." He folded his arms across his chest and waited.

After getting her laughter under control she gave him a smirk. "Did you hear yourself? 'Not on my watch.'" She did her best to mimic his deep masculine voice. It made her chuckle again briefly. "Who do you think you are? The Terminator? Things will happen. I got hurt because I disregarded your order to hide and instead joined the fight, so stop beating yourself up."

He was fighting back a smile when she finished. The adoring gaze he gave her never wavered as he pulled her onto his lap. "Maybe I should spank you for disregarding my order." His voice took on a seductive tone, and he arched a brow.

She licked her bottom lip while she looked at him, her eyes hooded with lust. "I have to warn you. I don't enjoy taking orders so you might have to punish me often." She gave him a wicked, wanton smile. Next thing she knew, she found herself facedown across his lap with her ass arched in the air, where he delivered stinging slaps alternated with gentle massages or kisses to soothe the offended area. The sensual spanking turned them both on. Round two lasted for hours before they both found themselves spent and sated.

"By the way, I love you too." She whispered before she fell asleep in his arms.

In the night, she rolled over onto her back away from Eli. A deep sleep was coming upon her and she found herself in a dream. It felt like the last dream she'd had, where she knew she was dreaming, but couldn't wake up from it. When she looked around, it was clear from the hallway she found herself in that she was back in Killian's castle. Why was she back here?

Fear took hold of her. She tried to crush it down, but found she was choking on it. Last time he couldn't see her. Only detect her presence. What if this time was different? She tiptoed down the long hallway and hoped and prayed she didn't meet up with anyone on her way to Killian's bedchamber. The female vampire from her dream and the attack flashed in her brain. She didn't want to run into her in this dream.

When she finally reached the door, she took a deep breath before quietly pushing the door open and stepping inside. The room was dimly lit. It appeared to be close to sunrise because the horizon was painted in subtle reds, oranges and pinks. She looked at the bed and saw a slight movement. Fight or flight kicked in. It was clear her body wanted to flee but there was a reason she was here and she had to know what it was.

Her feet carried her towards the bed. Terror at being caught wrapped itself like a hand around her throat. Still she continued to the bed. The closer she crept, the louder the sucking sound became. Her brows knit together in confusion. What was that?

After the longest, scariest walk to his bed, she still couldn't see what he was doing. The way his body was angled blocked out his actions. Slowly, she walked to the foot of the bed afraid of what she would find or witness. That's when she saw it.

It was Killian's true face. The horror of it froze her in place and terrified her. Dark red veins stood out in stark contrast under the pale skin around his eyes as the warm blood flooded his mouth. The cheekbones in his face had become angular and sharp. His eyes that were a dazzling green before were now jet-black. He no longer looked human, but exactly like the monster she always assumed he was. Blood dripped from the corners of his mouth while he fed on his victim, who she couldn't identify.

How much was he going to drain from them? They didn't even seem to struggle, just lay there limply. If she really wasn't here, she couldn't save them. Part of her couldn't understand why she wasn't running away. After another minute when he unlatched his fangs from the victim's throat, she walked around to their side of the bed so she could see who had been so unfortunate to wind up here.

Her eyes followed the trail his tongue made, licking the puncture wounds on the person's neck. She had to fight the urge to dry heave. When Killian leaned back, she stared at... herself. She was the victim. She was the one that lay in the bed with blood dribbling from the bite marks on her neck, her eyes open in a blank stare aimed at the ceiling. The revulsion and shock that gripped her left her catatonic and paralyzed. She watched in fascinated horror as Killian reached up and smoothed a few loose strands of hair. "Soon you'll be my companion." He whispered before his tongue licked up the side of her face.

Before she could shriek she came out of the dream and sat bolt upright from the bed gripping her chest. It felt like her heart was about to explode. Her heartbeat was so loud it was the only sound that penetrated her eardrums. After several frantic moments, she realized she was no longer in the dream and her fingers touched the flesh of her neck hoping to confirm it was still in one piece, that it didn't contain puncture marks, that it wasn't covered in her own blood.

"Willow?" Eli sat up beside her. The sheet slipped down and put his well-defined chest on display. Sleep tinged his voice. He rubbed his eyes and looked at the digital clock next to the bed. "Are you okay? Is it your wound? Does it hurt?" The concern on his face made her bite back the truth ready to fall from her lips. It was their first night together. The last thing she wanted was for Killian to ruin it and for Eli to be reminded of his duty.

"I'm okay." She reassured him with words while her mind raced and she screamed inside. Was it just a nightmare or did Killian have plans to turn her into an abomination? Had she seen what was to be her future? An uncontrollable shiver rippled through her body. "I'm just going to get a drink of water."

"You sure you don't want me to get it?" He offered.

"No, I got it. You go back to bed." She leaned over and kissed his mouth. He pulled her into his hard body and prolonged the kiss. He was such a good kisser. The heat level got turned up to a ten when his tongue swept in to explore the contours of her mouth. She was ready to forget the dream and all that it implied, but knew she needed to get up. With great regret she pushed against his chest to break the spell. She breathed against his mouth.

"Don't take too long." He panted, equally turned on. When he released her, she got up from the bed and slipped on his shirt. Upon first waking from the awful dream, she felt like there was something she needed to do. Now she had a clearer head and realized she was being drawn to her mother's letters. She hadn't thought about them since Cora gave them to her. She would read a couple.

When she looked back at the bed, he'd lay down again. Quickly she grabbed the letters from her bag and went into the bathroom. She shut the door and clicked on the light before sitting on the commode. Minutes passed while she held the bundle of yellowed envelopes. Some of her mother's last words were contained in these letters. Parts of her wanted to savor and prolong the reading, but the practical part of her knew there was information in the letters that might help them... help her ... figure out more about her abilities. Maybe her mother had seen more about her future. Her mind wandered back to tonight's dream, and she shivered again before pushing the memory away.

Once she untied the ribbon that held them together she rifled through them and found they were in order according to date. She grabbed the top envelope and slid her nail beneath the envelope seal. Her mother's scent wafted from the page as she pulled it out. Nearly twenty years had passed since her mother's death, but she'd never stopped missing her or remembering what she used to smell like. The mixture of rosehip oil, lavender and something that was uniquely her mother rose from the stationery. It was like she was holding a piece of her. Tears formed in the corners of her eyes.

> *Wednesday, May 15, 2002*
>
> *My dearest girl,*
>
> *There is so much I have learned. I want to prepare you for what's coming, but I fear you're too young right now. I'm writing this letter from Delphi, Greece. When you're old enough you must have Eli and the Protectors bring you here.*

Her eyes went wide after reading that line and a tear escaped. She swiped it away. Seeing her mother's prophecy of her being joined to Eli, and the Protectors made her belief in her Oracle powers even more real. The date on the letter indicated it was written only a few weeks before her mother's death.

What was she doing in Greece?
She continued reading the letter.

It is important you come because much will be revealed to you here. If Cora has done as I asked, you know the importance of this location to our ancestry. There's also something else you must know. There is something Killian wants besides you. He's also searching for The Book of Prophecy. It's a book that was passed down each generation since the original Oracle. The book holds prophecies and visions of each Oracle. Some of which haven't happened yet. It was lost to us, but now you must find it before he does.

You hold the key.

She looked up from the letter. What did her mother mean, 'She held the key?' A literal key? Or did she mean it figuratively? All she knew right now was that answers were waiting for her in Greece. Now she just had to convince the Protectors to take her there. Either way, with or without them she would find this book before Killian did and get some answers.

To Be Continued

***

Continue The Oracle Chronicles Series in the next novel, Enlightened.

www.moniboyce.com/series/oraclechronicles/

Keep up with Moni's releases by joining her newsletter!

www.moniboyce.com

Also By Moni Boyce:

Redemption of the Heart

ACKNOWLEDGMENTS

First and foremost, I want to thank God, because without him none of this would be possible. I'm grateful to have the time and means to do something I love and I love storytelling.

I want to acknowledge and thank my family and friends for always supporting and encouraging me. It means a lot to have them in my corner.

Thanks to my awesome beta readers: Jessica Thomas, Danielle Lynn and Angela Lee for their feedback that helped make the book even better. Thanks to Mallory from Rock Solid Design for the kickass cover she designed.

A really big thank you and shout out to all of my readers. You guys rock for buying and reading this book. I hope you enjoyed it enough to buy and read the next book in the series. I know there are lots of ways you could spend your money and your time and it means a lot that you chose to spend it reading my book. You have my gratitude.

What Did You Think of Awakened: The Oracle Chronicles?

First of all, thank you for purchasing this book **Awakened: The Oracle Chronicles.** *I know you could have picked any number of books to read, but you picked this book and for that I am extremely grateful.*

I hope that it added value and quality to your everyday life. If so, it would be really nice if you could share this book with your friends and family by posting to Facebook and Twitter.

If you enjoyed this book and found some benefit in reading this, I'd like to hear from you and hope that you could take some time to post a review. Your feedback and support will help me as an author to greatly improve my writing craft for future projects and make this book even better.

I want you, the reader, to know that your review is very important and so, if you'd like to **leave a review***, all you have to do is go to Amazon, Goodreads or Bookbub and leave a review. I wish you all the best in your future success!*

About the Author

Moni Boyce is a writer, filmmaker, poet and author of contemporary and paranormal romance. She spent the last fifteen years working in the film industry and now creates characters of her own and brings them to life on the page. Moni has ghostwritten romance novellas and novels for over a year now and decided to put some of her own creations out in the world. She considers herself a bookworm, film buff, foodie, music lover and an avid world traveler having visited 33 countries and counting. She lives a bit of a nomadic life, but considers Los Angeles home. Which is the subject of her first travel book: Greater Than A Tourist – Los Angeles, California: 50 Travel Tips From A Local. Learn more about her at www.moniboyce.com

http://www.facebook.com/MoniBoyceWrites
http://www.amazon.com/author/moniboyce
http://www.twitter.com/MoniBoyce
http://www.bookbub.com/authors/moni-boyce
http://www.goodreads.com/moniboyce

www.ingramcontent.com/pod-product-compliance
Lightning Source LLC
Chambersburg PA
CBHW021006120726

47905CB00009B/2883

9 780999 804367 8